The Casseveti Inheritance

Three siblings. Two families. One explosive will!

When billionaire James Casseveti dies, his business is split between the two children he abandoned from his first marriage and the daughter of his second. Siblings who've never even met! Can love reunite a family at war?

Ava Casseveti's father wants her to make amends for a wrong he did his former business partner. Will agreeing to help his son lead to a happy-ever-after?

Bitter at his father's betrayal, Luca Petrovelli has vowed never to fall in love. But can a marriage of convenience change his mind?

Overcome with grief, Jodie Petrovelli finds herself in the arms of her own Prince Charming. Can their secret baby unite them—forever?

Dear Reader,

This book was written during the very difficult times the world is going through.

As such, writing it was difficult but also joyous as it truly created a place I could escape to. And that is exactly what Luca and Emily do, too. Although they are supposedly on a work trip, their stay on the gorgeous fictional Indian island of Jalpura turns into an escape from real life. And in that bubble they start to truly be themselves, and despite all the many barriers and blockades they put up, they fall in love.

I hope you enjoy reading how love prevails and accompanies them back to the real world to ensure their happy-ever-after.

Nina x

Whisked Away by the Italian Tycoon

Nina Milne

HARLEQUIN®

Romance™

Recycling programs
for this product may
not exist in your area.

ISBN-13: 978-1-335-56704-8

Whisked Away by the Italian Tycoon

Copyright © 2021 by Nina Milne

All rights reserved. No part of this book may be used or reproduced in any manner whatsoever without written permission except in the case of brief quotations embodied in critical articles and reviews.

This is a work of fiction. Names, characters, places and incidents are either the product of the author's imagination or are used fictitiously. Any resemblance to actual persons, living or dead, businesses, companies, events or locales is entirely coincidental.

This edition published by arrangement with Harlequin Books S.A.

For questions and comments about the quality of this book, please contact us at CustomerService@Harlequin.com.

Harlequin Enterprises ULC
22 Adelaide St. West, 40th Floor
Toronto, Ontario M5H 4E3, Canada
www.Harlequin.com

Printed in U.S.A.

Nina Milne has always dreamed of writing for Harlequin Romance—ever since she played libraries with her mother's stacks of Harlequin romances as a child. On her way to this dream, Nina acquired an English degree, a hero of her own, three gorgeous children and—somehow!—an accountancy qualification. She lives in Brighton and has filled her house with stacks of books—her very own *real* library.

Books by Nina Milne

Harlequin Romance

The Casseveti Inheritance

Italian Escape with the CEO

A Crown by Christmas

Their Christmas Royal Wedding

Claiming His Secret Royal Heir
Marooned with the Millionaire
Conveniently Wed to the Prince
Hired Girlfriend, Pregnant Fiancée?
Whisked Away by Her Millionaire Boss
Baby on the Tycoon's Doorstep

Visit the Author Profile page
at Harlequin.com for more titles.

To Philippa—for being an amazing friend and for all the (socially distanced) support while I wrote this book

Praise for
Nina Milne

CHAPTER ONE

LUCA PETROVELLI SNAPPED his cufflink on. The simple design—a house that encompassed a cocoa bean—touched him with a familiar sense of pride. The logo represented his business—Palazzo di Cioccolato, an upmarket, growing chocolatier that Luca would one day take global.

Yet that ambition had been diluted, impacted by the death of his father. The man who had deserted him when Luca was only five years old. James Casseveti had left his pregnant wife and five-year-old son to marry another woman. An English aristocrat, with wealth and connections. His father had never looked back, had used the riches and contacts to set up his own company—Dolci, a dessert company that was a global success.

And as the young Luca had watched this success unfold, seen the glittering heights his father had reached, he'd made a vow. His success would surpass his father's and one day he would find James Casseveti and demonstrate that superiority. He'd been so close, planned to launch a new product and open a flagship London store, had envisaged hand-delivering the invitation to the glittering opening party. Tried to picture his father's face. The expression of surprise, shock, regret, pride... *No!* Luca didn't want his father to feel proud—he had no right.

In any case, now that would never happen. Because eight months ago James Casseveti had died, robbed him of that opportunity. Taken away Luca's chance for...revenge, justice, to ask the questions that had burned his childhood soul.

How could you leave me?
Why won't you see me?
What did I do wrong?

His own pride clicked in as he snapped the second cufflink. Of course, he would not have asked those questions, the idea of his father believing he gave a damn horrific. In any case he knew the answers, at some point he'd figured it out. There must have been something intrinsically wrong with Luca—after all, what parent left a child they truly loved, and then never came back, never so much as called or wrote or sent a postcard? He knew what his mother would say, had said, in fact—that it was nothing to do with Luca, that it was James Casseveti who was wrong. He could picture the fierce look on Therese Petrovelli's face as she said the words and Luca tried to believe her, told himself she was right, but deep down there was the sear of absolute certainty that the blame was his. A knowledge he'd worked to bury. To counter by a determination to show his father that he'd been wrong, that Luca had survived and thrived without him.

But now that couldn't happen and since James' death Luca had found himself in a state he did not recognise. Emotions strove to surface and he wanted none of them; he'd spent his life controlling his emotions, had long ago decided not to give his father the satisfaction of his feeling grief or anger or pain. So he'd subdued those emotions, then honed and focused them into a burning ambition and a desire for revenge.

A desire that had been thwarted and his conflict heightened by the irony of ironies that in death James had done what he hadn't done in life. Reached out to his first family. He'd left Luca and his sister, Jodi, a third share each in Dolci. With the remaining share going to his daughter from his second marriage, Ava Casseveti. A half-sister Luca had never even met, though he had followed her charmed, glittering life in the gossip columns—the life of an heiress-cum-supermodel-cum-businesswoman.

Then a month ago Ava had turned up unannounced to his business headquarters and forced a meeting. And to his surprise and chagrin there had been an instant sense of connection. Plus an admiration that she had gone against all advice and reached out to 'the enemy'. But despite the positivity of the experience Luca retained his natural wariness—instinct told him Ava was on the level, but experience told him to never show blind trust. Ava was James Casseveti's daughter, after all.

Yet here he was in a plush London hotel room, about to attend Ava's engagement party to celebrate her impending marriage to Liam Rourke. When he'd accepted the invitation he'd told himself it was a business decision. Dolci was floundering with the death of its founder and the uncertainty caused by the will. A show of unity would help calm the waters, and whilst a part of him didn't care if Dolci went under, he did care that it would take the livelihoods of many if it did.

But there was another reason he was here: a curiosity about this half-sister of his. For years he'd watched her grace the celebrity pages as an heiress, an aristocrat, and a model, the girl who had replaced him so comprehensively in his father's affections. The child James hadn't deserted. Hadn't left behind to face poverty, to endure the schoolyard bullies who had delighted in taunting the child whose father had 'desserted' him. Even now his fists clenched as he remembered the acrid taste of fear, the writhing sense of self-loathing because he was too weak to fight back. Along with the knowledge that the bullies were right—his father had abandoned him.

The father Luca had adored, looked up to… loved and never seen again. Yet Ava had had James in her life for twenty-seven years; for all her life she'd been loved and wanted. Innate justice told him it wasn't her fault and yet he couldn't help but wonder what did Ava possess that he didn't?

As if on cue there was a knock on the hotel-room door. 'Come in,' he called, even as he knew who it would be.

The door pushed open and—no surprise—Ava walked in, her amber eyes friendly but guarded. No doubt she was here to ensure he really would come downstairs, to attend the party due to start shortly.

Since their one meeting they had communicated by email and in that time Luca had worked hard to diminish any sense of kinship. After all, they might share a father but that did not make them family in a real sense. Luca's family was his mother and his sister and for them he would do anything. Ava was family in name only, by genetic mischance.

'Hey.' They said the word at the same time, and both smiled with the same degree of awkwardness.

Ava stepped forward and again there was the twinge of recognition, a familiarity that made little sense. 'I thought I'd check you were…'

'Here?' he asked, the quip half in earnest. 'I told you I would attend—I do not break my word.'

'Actually, I was going to say OK. I came to see if you were OK. I know you don't particularly want to be here. So I wanted to thank you because it is my engagement party and I want my brother to be here.' Her gaze met his with more than a hint of challenge and against his will he found himself admiring her stance. He knew it took guts to admit that, knew too that she felt deep regret for her father's actions and he wished he knew what to say.

Ava must have sensed his turmoil—not hard as a quick glance at his reflection showed a terrifying scowl etched his face. One he attempted to replace with a rictus of a smile and, perhaps emboldened by this, Ava inhaled deeply and continued. 'I wish Jodi could be here too. Have you heard from her?'

'No.' His voice was clipped as the ever-present worry resurfaced. After James' death Jodi had thrown in her job and gone travelling. At first she had stayed in touch, kept him apprised of her travels through Thailand and India. Had been excited to visit the Indian island of Jalpura, home to the cocoa farm that Palazzo di Cioccolato had recently signed up to provide beans for a new product. Whilst there she'd got involved with the Royal Film Festival held on the same island. But her communications had changed, become briefer and at longer intervals. She'd sounded *different*. Then two months ago she'd said she needed some space and she'd be in touch soon. Whatever that meant. Had made him promise not to try and find her, do anything 'dramatic' or go into 'overprotective overdrive'.

Ava moved a little closer. 'I know you're worried, but Jodi has told you she is OK. Given everything, it's understandable she wants space.'

'Yes.' But Luca knew that wasn't true. Because he knew his sister and this was not like her. To shut him out. Something was going on— he knew it, suspected Jodi was in trouble. But this was nothing to do with Ava. Jodi's feelings about their half-sister were even more ambiguous than his own and so he only told Ava the minimum, just enough to explain why he couldn't make any decisions about what to do about his share in Dolci.

Nodding, he forced a smile to his face. 'I am sure you are right.' Then, wanting to change the subject, 'Thank you for your email with the guest list.' Ava had sent him the list along with details about 'friendly faces'. Something he appreciated but didn't need. Luca had no qualms about his ability to navigate a social gathering, even if it would contain people who didn't like him. People who resented the fact he and Jodi now controlled Dolci. And as he looked at Ava he realised that this woman, the one who had the most right to resent them, didn't. Was actually concerned about his welfare. Almost against his will the knowledge touched him.

'No problem. I thought it would help.'

Luca smiled. 'It will. Do not worry about me, Ava. Enjoy your party, be happy.'

'I am happy.' Now her smile was radiant. 'Truly happy.'

'I'm glad.' And part of him was, though it went against the grain to wish happiness upon this half-sister he did not know how to feel about. If only he could simply decide to hate her, to transfer his anger at his father to this woman. But he couldn't, knew it was not Ava who had done wrong. 'I will see you later. At the party.'

Emily Khatri looked round the glitter of the ballroom, the theme of love clear in the setting.

Candles, white flowers intertwined with red, the pop of champagne corks and the background strains of the orchestra. And for a second a tiny taste of bitterness invaded her. Because for a brief period she had believed in love and romance and happy ever after, allowed herself to be deluded, conned into a belief in fairy tales.

Well, no more. Her marriage had been a disaster of epic proportions and had ended in betrayal and misery. Remembered grief over her miscarriage twisted inside her, the grief made even worse by its lateness, at a time when she had believed her baby to be safe, had felt him kick inside her. On instinct she placed a hand over her now flat belly, remembered the swell of pregnancy, and she closed her eyes to ward away the pain as a stab of sadness hit her heart.

A sadness she had borne alongside the sheer humiliation of the discovery during her pregnancy that her husband had been having an affair.

Enough. The all too familiar haunt of guilt threatened. If she and Howard hadn't had a row over his infidelity would she still have lost the baby? Had the miscarriage been caused by the emotional fallout? Been caused by any action of hers? *Not now.* Those questions had hammered at her incessantly. She had spent months in an abyss of misery and despair, one she had slowly and excruciatingly pulled herself out of. This was a happy occasion and she would embrace it. For Ava's sake if not her own, she could and would still be happy for her best friend. Ava literally glowed and there was no way Emily would rain on her parade.

Plus it was time to get her life back together, to try and barricade against the might-have-beens, the gut-wrenching knowledge that right now she should be holding her baby in her arms. That was not to be; all she could now do was throw herself back into work.

Though that was proving easier said than done; so far all her efforts had been to no avail and now anxiety threw itself into the emotional churn. Because it seemed as though her marriage to and divorce from Howard had alienated a whole load of people. Howard's pernicious influence made itself felt as people she had believed to be friends avoided her calls and emails. Perhaps she shouldn't be surprised that people had taken Howard's part so readily. Howard, of globally renowned fame, winner of numerous awards and accolades for his hard-hitting photography from all over the world. Howard, presenter of wildly successful documentaries, Howard in talk with Hollywood producers… As such her ex wielded a whole heap of influence, had a network of friends in high places ready to believe him or make excuses for him. And in the aftermath of the miscarriage Emily hadn't cared about anything, had left the field to Howard, who had spun rumours and lies and somehow made himself out to be the hero of the hour, a persecuted husband who had done his best. After that sheer pride had prevented her from even attempting to tell her side of the story; she would not use her miscarriage to garner sympathy.

The only silver lining was that they had never announced her pregnancy—Howard had decreed it to be a private thing. Hadn't wanted it to distract from his imminent book launch, or so he'd said. When there had been speculation in the press he had denied it, without so much as consulting her. Turned out it was because he didn't want the other woman he was sleeping with to find out; he'd been lying to her as well.

Not that she would deign to try to prove that it was Howard who had been the cheat and the liar. She suspected that no one would believe her if she did. Instead she'd decided to somehow put it all behind her and tonight she would try the face-to-face approach, see if she could talk her way into a job.

Yet for a debilitating moment as she looked out at the crowd panic rooted her to the spot, stretched its tendrils round her nerves, caused her heart to pound against her ribcage and her breathing to turn shallow. Oh, God. Not now. Ever since the miscarriage panic assailed her, held her hostage at a whim, but she'd thought she'd tamed it, or at least learnt to hold it at bay.

But this was her first public foray, her first attempt to navigate the real world and she wasn't sure she could manage it. Especially without the comfort of her camera in her hand to hide behind; she missed its familiar shape, the protective mantle of invisibility it threw over her. People tended to only see the lens, not the person behind it, and tonight she hated feeling so visible. *Enough*; she forced herself to move forward, hoped, prayed that if she launched into the fray she would stave off the panic before it took hold. One blind step, straight into the path of a fellow guest.

Instinctively she put out a hand to balance herself, the high-heeled shoes an added liability, and her palm landed on an arm. An arm hard with muscle under the super-soft fabric of his tuxedo.

'Sorry.' She let go, nearly leapt backwards.

'It is I who should apologise. I did not see you behind the pillar.'

As she looked up at the owner of the Italian-tinged voice, *Wow* sprang to the forefront of her brain and flashed in neon. This man was seriously gorgeous. Obsidian-black hair, a little bit overlong with a rebellious spikiness. Silver-grey eyes, a face that demonstrated strength, the nose a broad arrogant jut, the jaw square and determined. His body was solid muscle packed into a beautifully cut tux that moulded to said muscles.

Emily blinked, realised the wow factor had derailed her. Completely. On the plus side the hormonal surge seemed to have also shocked panic into retreat. *Say something.*

'I was just…' *looking at your muscles* '…preparing to enter the fray.' *Really, Emily? Great opener.*

'So this evening is a battle? An ordeal?' There was a hint of amusement in his voice but for a mad moment she also sensed an empathy.

'No. Of course not. I am thrilled to be here to celebrate such a happy occasion.'

'But?'

'There is no but. Or at least… I guess I am a little nervous. I haven't been on the social scene that much recently and…' And now she needed to stop talking. 'Anyway…'

'Let me introduce myself.' The deep Italian-tinged voice sent a trickle of warmth straight through her even as her brain registered its meaning and finally managed to put two and two together. His identity clicked as he held out his hand. 'I am Luca Petrovelli.'

Of course—clearly her brain had turned to mush. The accent should have alerted her as soon as he spoke and, now she knew, she could see some elusive fleeting resemblance to Ava. Though she wasn't sure how or where—Ava was blonde, beautiful and an ex-supermodel. Luca's hair was midnight dark and his face was all lines and planes, his body all muscle. Solid, compact breadth of muscle. There was that word again and this was ridiculous. Her interest in the opposite sex was currently non-existent; her libido had buried itself under layers, strata of misery. Yet this man had poleaxed her. Comprehensively.

And she still hadn't shaken hands. 'I'm Emily.'

Luca's brow creased for a second. 'I know we haven't met, but you look familiar.'

Emily sighed. She was used to this, even when she omitted giving her surname, as was her wont. People 'knew' her because of her parentage—because she was the daughter of Marigold Turner and Rajiv Khatri. One of the world's most iconic models and a Bollywood film star respectively. Emily was the product of their brief marriage. Clearly brief ill-fated marriages ran in the family. At least on her mother's side. Marigold was currently on husband number five; Emily would have the sense to stop at one. Alternatively, Luca might know her because of Howard.

'It's likely something to do with my parents or maybe my ex.'

As she said the words he snapped his fingers. 'Got it! I visited the Dolci head offices this morning. I think Ava has a photo of you in her collage of photos on the wall.'

Oh. 'Sorry. I am so used to people asking me about my famous parents or what it feels like to have been married to a genius that I assumed that's why you would recognise me.' After all, why else would he?

'In which case, I promise not to ask any of those questions. Tell me instead how you met Ava.' Surprise touched her—Luca wasn't even going to ask who her parents were, though, thinking about it, she supposed it was natural for Luca to ask about Ava. They were siblings, however complicated the situation was.

'A few years ago, back when Ava was a model, I was one of the fashion photographers on her shoot. We just clicked.'

Now he smiled and Emily blinked. The man had already awoken her long dormant hormones—now his smile had them doing aerobics. 'It's good when you just click,' he said, and his voice deepened to a rumble that slid over her skin. Was he flirting? Could she blame him?

Somehow, without even noticing, she seemed to have closed the gap between them, was, oh, so close, too close. Near enough that the expensive hint of his soap tickled her nostrils, close enough that she could see the faintest hint of five o'clock shadow, study the thick gloss of his dark hair. And again her thought processes were derailed. Quickly she stepped backward.

'Yes. Yes, it is. What do you think makes people click?' No, no, no. That had come out all wrong. Now it sounded as if *she* were flirting. Was she? What was happening? How and why was this man affecting her so powerfully? She could almost feel more of her hormones yawn and stretch as they woke up for the first time in months. She ploughed on hurriedly. 'With Ava and me, we shared a sense of humour, found it easy to talk to each other, so we grabbed a coffee together and then it snowballed from there.'

'I agree a sense of humour is important and, of course, ease of conversation. For friendship *or* any sort of relationship. Though, of course, other things are important too.'

'Such as?'

'First impressions. A sense of instant connection. In a relationship, mutual attraction.'

'Pah!' The noise somewhere between a snort of derision and a puff of exasperation left her lips and he raised his eyebrows.

'Pah?' he repeated.

'Yes. You are talking about how a person looks.' Her mother had been feted and glorified for her beauty. Men tumbled head over heels for Marigold Turner but it never lasted, no relationship ever made it past the attraction—once reality kicked in they slowly faded away. Yet with every man Marigold waxed lyrical about 'instant attraction', 'magnetic pull' and, of course, 'love at first sight'.

Hell, Emily could date her childhood years by husbands' number two to four. At the start of each 'magical romance' Marigold had 'known' this was 'the one' and Emily had been relegated, encouraged to fade to the background of her mother's life. Remembered pain at the sense of isolation, the hurt at knowing she was seen as an obstacle, tingled inside her.

'Darling, I need you to keep out of the way. I don't want Kevin to think you're a nuisance.'

'Sorry, sweetheart, I know I promised I'd read you a bedtime story...come to Sports Day...but Alex is more important.'

Yet when each relationship ended in the slam of the door as each husband left, Marigold would turn to her daughter for solace and comfort and Emily would help pick up the pieces of her mother's shattered heart. Time and again 'instant attraction' had translated to 'later misery'.

Now she glared at Luca. 'Looks don't matter.'

'I disagree. First impressions count. Do you not judge people by the way they dress or the way they cut their hair or…?'

The size of their muscles? asked a small sly inner voice that she shushed instantly.

'Of course, I don't. Because if you get all caught up in that you forget what is important. And that's what is inside. Attraction isn't enough to make a relationship work. Not in the long term.' Her father's second marriage was proof of that. Neela was the antithesis to his first wife; she wasn't beautiful, just…ordinary and the marriage had been content. They had five children and she knew her dad was happy. So happy that Emily felt a bit redundant. Someone he'd seen once or twice a year during her childhood, and during those visits Emily had felt out of place. In the hurly burly rough and tumble of a real family life, she'd been an invisible outsider, an extra accorded a politeness due to a guest.

But that was beside the point. 'Attraction is too…distracting.' Which presumably explained why her gaze continued to dwell on the breadth of his chest, the lithe swell of his forearm, the clean strength of his jawline. If she could kick herself, she would.

Luca watched her carefully and now his lips tipped up, his grey eyes lit with a hint of amusement. 'A happy distraction, or a start point—that initial spark is…exhilarating.'

'I…' Now their gazes seemed to mesh; her lips went suddenly dry and it felt as though the edges of the world fuzzed, to leave only Luca and Emily in the room. Madness. But, mad or not, she couldn't seem to break free of the sheer tug of desire that pulled her feet, urged them to move closer to him. 'I suppose so.'

She forced herself to break the gaze only to find herself focused on his lips, firm, strong and such a defined shape. She'd never studied the shape of a man's lips before, the contours, never wanted to touch, to smooth her fingers over a mouth.

Enough. There was going to be no clicking of any kind going on. 'So,' she said. 'I guess it's time to circulate.'

'To enter the fray,' he said in echo of her earlier words.

'Yes.' Reluctance gripped her and without meaning to she sighed. Once again she wished she had a camera with her to render her invisible.

'You have no need to be nervous.' The nerves

she'd alluded to, the nerves that had completely vanished during their conversation. Replaced by the cartwheel of her hormones, the spark of attraction and the sparkle of an interesting conversation with an undercurrent of simmer. A happy distraction indeed.

'I think I do. There are a lot of people out there with a preconceived opinion of me, who have already made judgement.' Her voice was imbued with a hint of bitterness as she scanned the room. Recalled the number of people who had already avoided her emails and calls.

'Does it matter?' His tone was serious now. 'Surely the only people whose opinions matter are the people you care about. And who care about you.'

In theory that held good, but, 'You're right. I know you are, but when I see the pity or the judgement in people's faces I...'

'Crumble inside a little?' he offered.

'Yes.' How did Luca know? And how on earth had this conversation with a stranger got so personal? The idea sent unease through her—no way should she be sharing on a personal level with a complete stranger, even if he was Ava's half-brother. In this case *especially* because he was Ava' s half-brother.

'When you feel like that you need to remember it is their problem, not yours. Show them they are wrong. Wrong to pity you and wrong in their judgement.' There was a resonance in his voice and a shadow crossed his features. Then, as if he too sensed that the conversation had edged into deep waters, he shrugged and there came that smile again. 'It also helps to imagine the people you are most worried about making silly faces or dressed in absurd costumes. Or in embarrassing situations.'

'Do you do that?'

'Absolutely.'

Now she chuckled. 'Is that what you are going to do now?' It sounded as if he spoke from experience, yet she couldn't imagine this man being worried by anyone.

'If need be, absolutely. I am sure there are plenty of people out there who have judged me too, as the evil villain, the usurper of the Dolci inheritance.'

'Ava doesn't believe that.' She knew her best friend didn't hold Luca to blame at all.

'Perhaps, perhaps not. But either way I am here to try to help further Dolci business interests. But now I have also had the pleasure of meeting you.' He smiled and held out his hand. 'I wish you luck in the fray.'

'Th…' She placed her hand in his and bit back a small gasp, told herself that electricity could not be generated by touch. Yet she saw an an-

swering awareness flicker in his eyes. Her hand
remained in his and for one mad second she
wondered if he would kiss it in some quixotic
gesture of gallantry. The idea tingled her skin
and of their own volition her feet took a step
closer to him.

The noise of a throat clearing broke the spell
and she pulled away her hand as Luca let go and
they turned towards the man who now stood
next to them. Emily flushed as she realised she
hadn't even noticed his approach.

'Liam,' she said hurriedly as she moved towards Ava's fiancé, kissed him on one cheek
and then stood back. She had a lot of time for
Liam, knew him to be a good, honourable man
who truly loved her best friend. 'It's lovely to
see you.'

Was there a glint of speculation in his eyes
as he glanced from Luca to her? She could only
hope not as she watched the two men shake
hands, sensed the wariness in Luca's stance.
Knew from Ava that the two men had only met
once, that it had been Liam who had taken Luca
around Dolci headquarters that morning.

'Ava asked me to tell you her mum has arrived, and she wondered if you want to get the
introductions out of the way sooner rather than
later.'

Now Luca's wariness froze into something

Emily couldn't identify, though she imagined his feelings could only be negative about Karen Casseveti, the woman who had supplanted his own mother. As for Karen, it was well known that she couldn't stand Luca or his sister, Jodi. So this meeting wouldn't be welcome to either.

'Of course,' Luca said.

'I'll leave you to it…'

'Actually no,' Liam intervened. 'Ava thought it may look more natural if we mingle as a group. If you both don't mind?'

Luca hesitated and then gave a decisive nod. 'That makes sense. If that is OK with Emily.'

'Of course.' Emily knew how good her friend was at orchestrating publicity and managing social occasions. 'I'm happy to help.'

'Then let's go,' Luca said.

CHAPTER TWO

Luca concentrated on keeping his expression neutral; this was a moment he had known would come. The meeting with Ava's mother, the woman who had taken James Casseveti away. It was not Karen Casseveti's fault, he reminded himself; it had been his father's choice to walk away, his father's choice to not even visit his children from his first marriage, to paint them out of his new life. Yet it was impossible not to feel some animosity.

Probably best to focus on something else, or perhaps someone, and a person came all too easily to mind. Emily, the woman at his side. From the minute he'd seen her he'd been a little on edge, a little too aware of her. Too caught up in her smile, the elusive scent, and the ripples of awareness, the undeniable tug and pull of attraction. One he'd do best to douse. Emily was Ava's best friend; that put her strictly out of bounds. It was all complicated enough. But still his curiosity was piqued. Why did she see this crowd as a fray? Why hadn't she been on the social scene for a while?

And in the here and now he could feel the warmth of her body next to him, and somehow it helped as they made their way through the throng of people—Emily's own reluctance to 'enter the fray' made her feel like an ally.

One he was in need of as they approached their destination and anger surged and simmered inside him. *Grow up, Petrovelli.*

Luca tried to remember his own mother's advice. 'Do not show anger or hatred or bitterness, Luca. This woman is much to be pitied right now. She has lost her husband and in truth I am not sure she ever had him.' His mother had shown him the letter she had received on James Casseveti's death, a letter etched on Luca's memory.

Dear Therese,
I am sorry...
    Sorry I behaved as I did.
    Please know I have thought of you every day since I left and never stopped loving you. I know I did wrong, and sometimes I imagine the life we could have had...wonder if I could have started Dolci with you by my side, or whether that even matters.

*I gained wealth and business success but
I lost you. As I have grown older I realise
that in the end I also lost out. On watching our children grow up, on growing old
with a woman I truly love.*

*All I can do now is to try and make
amends with an apology to you and by
leaving Luca and Jodi a legacy.*
James

As he'd read the words, he had felt a surge
of protective love for her, laced with anger at
James. An apology that was too little, too late
because Therese had never got over her husband's desertion. She'd tried a few relationships
but had never been able to commit. He'd heard
her once tell a man that she couldn't put herself, couldn't put her children through the possibility of another break-up. Not unless she was
sure it was really worth it, and she couldn't see
that any man was.

Turned out no woman was worth it either. His
own first and only love had left him for a man
more sophisticated and wealthy than Luca. A
repeat of history with a twist. The lesson rein-
forced: people he loved abandoned him. Wealth
and position trumped love. Always. An image
of Lydia shimmered into his brain and he ban-
ished it. All she had been was proof that love

was a crock—nothing was worth that level of pain if you lost it.

Per carità, Luca. Not now, for goodness' sake. This was not the moment to dwell on the past; as the thought crossed his mind he was aware of the gentlest of nudges from next to him. 'You OK?' Emily's voice was whisper thin.

'I'm fine.'

'Good. You've got this.'

He glanced across at her and she smiled and for an instant the word 'arrested' took on new meaning; this woman literally stunned him. Shoulder-length straight hair, near black with a tinge of chestnut highlight, flawless brown skin and eyes with a depth of umber. Her nose gave her face character, her mouth generous. Then even as his brain registered bedazzlement her expression morphed and he blinked as she crossed her eyes and stuck out the tip of her tongue.

His puzzlement switched to instant understanding, her funny face a reminder of his own words from earlier—in a difficult situation imagine whoever is giving you grief pulling a silly face or in an embarrassing position. Now he couldn't help but smile back at her, warmed by her gesture of solidarity and a strange sense of camaraderie, given she didn't even know him.

He braced himself as they approached Ava

and Karen; Ava stood next to her mother and he could see the family likeness, though he could also see an unsettling resemblance in Ava to his sister Jodi. Suddenly he wished Jodi were here by his side, instead of God knew where after her trip to Jalpura. *Not now.* He'd figure out what to do about Jodi later. Plus his sister would hate this gathering with every iota of her being. Edginess lined his gut as he forced his lips into a parody of an upturn.

'Luca, this is my mum, Karen. Mum, this is Luca.'

He managed to keep the smile in place and although he saw the swiftly veiled venom in the older woman's eyes, to her credit her return smile was faultless, before she turned to Emily. 'Hello, Emily. It is good to see you again.'

'And you, Mrs Casseveti. Especially at such a happy occasion.'

'Yes.' The word was said with emphasis, yet the warmth felt cloying in its falsity and he knew that if these were medieval times he would suspect a poisoned chalice at the table.

With that Ava managed to launch the conversation into fashion and Luca swiftly turned to Liam and asked about business, the next ten minutes an orchestration in small talk that successfully minimised contact between Karen and Luca whilst giving the interested guests a show of unity. A necessity to show the world that Dolci was still viable. The knowledge enabled him to play along until finally the strains of the orchestra announced the first dance. Gave them all an out. He turned to Ava. 'Perhaps if you and Liam and Emily and I head to the dance floor together for the first dance it would be a further demonstration of *family* unity.' And if the word 'family' held more than a tint of bitterness he didn't care. Took satisfaction from Karen's barely perceptible wince.

A hesitation and then Ava nodded. 'Good idea,' she said, and the four of them headed to the dance floor as Karen's attention was claimed by another guest.

'I hope this *is* OK,' he said to Emily.

'Of course. I know how important it is to show that you and Ava are working together and I know people are watching.'

'Yes. Absolutely.' Problem was that wasn't actually why he'd suggested it—he'd *wanted* to dance with Emily. Wanted to hold her in his arms, wanted to continue their conversation, find out more about her. The depth of the desire triggered a sense of alarm, as he realised just how much this woman had hit him bang between the eyes. This was not a good idea on many levels. Emily was Ava's best friend; every word he said to her would be filtered back, possibly analysed and discussed. The idea brought his eyebrows together in a frown. Equally he had little doubt that Ava would be super protective of her friend, which would complicate an already complicated situation.

Chill, Luca. He wasn't planning on proposing to Emily—one dance could do no harm. 'So I guess we'd better get on there.'

Doubt widened her dark brown eyes for an instant, almost as if it was only now the real dangers had occurred to her. Before either of them could change their mind he stepped forward and pulled her into his arms.

He held in a gasp, heard Emily's intake of breath and tried to regulate his own breathing. The scent of her shampoo tickled his nose, the span of his hand on her waist, seemed to suck the air from his lungs. The soft silky sheen of her dress, her sheer closeness and warmth played mayhem with his senses as the haunting notes of the melody lingered in the air.

And she felt it too, he knew it, could see it as she lifted her gaze to his, surprise in the depths of her deep brown eyes, her lips rounded in a small circle as she moved a step closer, her body swaying in a natural rhythm with his. Now surprise morphed to awareness and he could see a desire that matched his own. And now his entire focus was on Emily, the two of them lost in the moment, so attuned that they barely even needed the music.

As the dance continued she moved even nearer, her body now, oh, so close, her arms looped round his neck and she looked up at him, lips parted, and he knew he wanted to kiss her, knew she wanted it too and his head spun; every instinct urged him to lower his head and meet her lips. Until a small alarm of self-preservation pealed, told him that if he kissed this woman he would step over the edge of an abyss.

Break this spell, whatever it is.

But how? Somehow he had to inject some form of normalcy, to ward off this insidious desire. 'So you're a photographer?' It was all he could think of to say and his tongue twisted around the words, but he could see the relief on her face that he'd instigated any form of conversation. Even as he could see and empathise with her struggle to formulate an answer, and wondered if, like himself, Emily felt as though she were emerging from a fog of desire.

'Yes.' A pause as she straightened her spine and gave her head a small shake as if to clear her brain. 'Yes. I am. Ready and available.' Now her eyes closed momentarily and she gave a small groan. 'For work, I mean. Obviously. What else could I mean? Don't answer that.' Her inhalation was audible as she moved a little further from him within the movement of the dance. 'I meant I took a…a sabbatical for a year and a half but now I'm looking for work. Really looking. My plan tonight is to network.'

Luca heard the hesitation, the small catch in her throat when she mentioned a sabbatical, wondered what had made her step away from a successful career path. If she had been involved in Ava's shoots, he had little doubt her credentials would be A grade. His half-sister had graced the cover of the world's top magazines as well as modelled for exclusive brands. Yet Emily had taken time out, and now as she surveyed the crowd of guests he sensed her anxiety was real. 'With the fray?' he asked.

'Exactly.'

'Surely you could contact all your old clients.'

'Yes. But unfortunately it's not that easy.' Her voice was clipped now, and he sensed a simmer of frustration.

'Why not?' It was true that he wasn't supposed to be curious but, hell, curiosity had at least down-notched the attraction factor. Plus he wanted to know what had brought that frown to her brow.

'I am a bit persona non grata in the industry at present.'

As she spoke the music came to an end and Luca guided her off the dance floor as a matter of priority, before he succumbed to the temptation of keeping her in his arms for the next dance. Knew that now was the perfect moment to separate, to say, *Thank you for the dance. I'll let you go and network. Good luck.*

But his brain and his voice had some sort of mix-up and instead he found himself saying, 'Why is that? Why don't we go and sit down and you can tell me? *Then* you can go and network.' Told himself there was no harm to it. In two days he would be on a plane home. Back to Italy. So surely it didn't matter if they helped each other get through a difficult evening. He gestured to a small table partly shielded by a pillar and a luscious large-leaved plant. 'Shall we?'

It was a good question. For the second time Emily hesitated—was this a good idea? *Should they* go and sit together in a secluded corner? After a dance that had nearly caused her to spontaneously combust. Yes, yelled her hormones. But it wasn't only her hormones. It was so long since she had felt attractive, that someone was genuinely interested in her, and the knowledge fizzed adrenalin through her body. Howard had been the master of the understated barb, had an uncanny ability to undermine her confidence, and she'd been on tenterhooks the entire time she was with him. Had despised herself for craving his approval but had found herself desperately seeking it nonetheless.

Tonight for the first time since she had fallen pregnant, lost her baby, gone through the pain of discovering Howard's infidelity and the strain and misery of the divorce, for the first time in month upon month she felt a little lighter.

So perhaps in the here and now she should take a few moments of light with this drop-dead gorgeous stranger. Perhaps she could harness the confidence boost into networking successfully. Perhaps she would even feel better if she explained the situation to someone not involved, someone she wouldn't see again after tonight.

'After you,' she said now and followed him towards the table, allowed her eyes to linger on the breadth of his back, the width of his shoulders, the sheer compact muscular strength of him impossible to ignore.

Once seated she sipped from the glass of champagne he'd taken from a passing waiter.

'So,' he said. 'Tell me what the problem is?'

Emily considered. No way was she telling Luca the whole story. Her grief, the pain, the misery and humiliation were still too raw to share with anyone, let alone a complete stranger who had no reason to give a damn.

'The problem is I married a man who has a huge amount of clout in the magazine and entertainment industry. Our divorce was a bit acrimonious and as a result people are choosing not to employ me, or are ignoring my emails.'

'Who is your ex?'

'Howard McAllister.'

Luca raised his eyebrows. 'I have heard of him. He did a phenomenally successful TV series. My sister loved it.'

'That's him. He has also won numerous photography awards, is in talks with Hollywood about a film and is feted and adored by all and sundry. Hence I am not flavour of the month.'

His frown held a fierceness. 'That does not seem fair. Could you not call people out on this?'

'There is no point. No one has come straight out and said that's why there is no available work for me. They have other plausible reasons: I've been off the scene for too long, my skills aren't quite the fit they need for a particular project, blah blah blah.'

'Could your parents help? You said they are famous—are they part of the fashion industry?'

'I'd rather not get a job just because they demand it for me.' That was matter of principle. All her life she'd loathed being courted or feted simply because of her parents' fame and status—no way would she use that. Emily had vowed from a young age that she would stand on her own two feet, come what may. At some point she had realised that she wasn't necessary to her parents, that they didn't love her in the same way other parents loved their children.

They didn't abuse or dislike her, indeed they were quite fond of her, but both would have been perfectly happy if she had never been born, a reminder of their disastrous brief romance. Marigold Turner didn't have a maternal bone in her body; her primary concern was the pursuit of love and keeping her looks. Her father's priority was his second family, the five children he lived with, the product of a successful union.

So Emily had decided to accept her place in the pecking order, but had also vowed to make her own way in life, find her own niche, without using her parents' fame or wealth. 'Using them seems just as wrong as people not giving me a job because I'm Howard's ex-wife.'

'That is not so. Are you a good photographer? I am assuming you are, given you worked with Ava on a number of shoots.'

Emily opened her mouth to assert that she was good, but the words wouldn't come. Instead an image of Howard flitted across her mind; his voice rang in her head, belittling her portfolio as 'good if you can count that sort of thing as real photography'. Gritting her teeth, she pushed the memory away. Her photography, her career, was one thing she did have, the one area of her life where she could hold her own and her head high. She might never reach the pinnacle of her profession, or transition to serious photography, never have Howard's stature, but, 'I'm good. I worked on shoots for *Theme*, *Star's Market* and *Genie*, all top fashion magazines.'

'Then use what influence you have, use your parents. If you are being discriminated against you should use every weapon you have. All you are doing is fighting fire with fire.'

'Perhaps. But all my life I have been known as the daughter of Marigold Turner and Rajiv Khatri. I will not use my name or their status— I want to stand on my own two feet.'

His whole body stilled. 'Your father is Rajiv Khatri, the Bollywood actor?' An expression she couldn't interpret flitted over his face and she frowned. Usually people were more interested in the fact she was Marigold Turner's daughter.

'Yes. He's a superstar in India, though not that many European people have heard of him.' She tilted her head to one side. 'Obviously you have?'

'Yes.'

She waited but that appeared to be it. Though she sensed he wasn't being rude, just distracted.

'How? Have you seen one of his films?'

'No.' As if realising how abrupt he'd been he shrugged. 'Sorry. It is not a very interesting story. As you may know, I founded a chocolate company, Palazzi di Cioccolato. A year ago I found a new source for cocoa beans. On the Indian island of Jalpura.'

Now she understood. Jalpura hosted a biannual film festival that showcased both Indian and European films. 'My father is pretty popular on Jalpura.'

'Yes.' But somehow she suspected there was more to it than that. 'Has he ever attended the festival?'

'Once, I believe, a few years ago.' She'd read an article about his trip—'Rajiv Khatri and his family attended the festival…' The words had held a barb—he hadn't even asked her, had taken his second wife and their five children. She knew she was being oversensitive—those children lived with him; she had been in her mid-twenties; he would have taken her if she'd asked—but for some reason it still stung. The knowledge she wasn't really family. 'The island looks beautiful, a photographer's dream.'

'It is also a chocolatier's heaven. The cocoa beans were an amazing find—we are about to launch a whole new brand.'

A whole new brand of chocolate; the idea piqued her interest, as did the note of determination and enthusiasm in his voice. 'How does that work? I take it the beans taste different? Make a completely different-tasting chocolate?'

'Well, a potted version is that, yes, different beans do definitely create distinctive tastes— because of climate, processing and sometimes, I believe, the personality of the grower. I may be being whimsical but I always prefer beans grown by people I like, with fair value and work practices and ethos.' He shook his head. 'But that is obviously not even remotely scientific.'

'No, but I think you're right. Creativity and growth come from inside. It sounds like the beans are really important to your brand.' She tucked a strand of hair behind her ear as ideas sparked her professionalism. 'Maybe you should use photos of them in your promotional material. Or have some sort of documentary on your website? About Jalpura—it sounds like a fascinating place. Complete with a royal family— you could even have a fairy-tale theme. Beauty and the Bean'

She stopped, she could almost hear the whir of his brain before he gave a long slow smile. 'You're a genius.'

'I am?'

'You are. Tell me, would you like a job?'

CHAPTER THREE

LUCA BARELY REGISTERED Emily's look of confusion, his brain too busy running with its brilliant plan. Because Emily's suggestion was advertising genius and it had sparked an idea in his head. He could plan an advertising campaign to launch his new brand and shoot it on Jalpura—Emily was right, it was a magical location and the source of the bean that had inspired the chocolate. The campaign also presented him with a legitimate reason for going to Jalpura and whilst there he could discreetly retrace Jodi's footsteps, figure out what had changed his sister and where the hell she was now. So far so good.

And Emily was the perfect person for the job—she had come up with the concept and it made sense for her to run with it, she was immediately available, she had the skills he needed and she needed a job. Plus, as an added bonus, she was the daughter of Rajiv Khatri, Bollywood star, and therefore holder of hero status on Jalpura. If he needed to talk to anyone associated with the Royal Film Festival her name would open every door. But would Emily be willing to do that? She'd been adamant that she didn't like using her name to gain advantage. But this was different—this wasn't to help herself, it was to help Jodi.

The obvious thing to do would be to ask her. Problem was he knew Jodi would loathe her business being told to anyone. Especially Ava's best friend. Yet the idea of asking Emily to do a job without full disclosure didn't sit well with him.

Belatedly his radar kicked in and he realised that his wannabe travel partner had no idea what he was talking about.

'A job?' she asked. 'What sort of job?'

Luca made a decision. For now he'd leave Jodi out of it. For a start Emily might not even take the job, second he might not need to use her name. Therefore he'd keep the Jodi angle out of it. For now. 'I love the Beauty and the Bean idea and I want to go with it. Shoot the ad campaign on Jalpura. To launch the brand.'

'Just like that?'

'Yup. What do you think?'

'I don't think anything because it makes no sense.' Her voice was tight. 'Why would you offer me a job when you haven't even seen a portfolio of my work? Or a single picture I have taken? When I am a *fashion* photographer?' Emily rose to her feet. 'I am sorry if I gave you the wrong impression, but I am not interested in whatever it is you have in mind.'

Oh, hell. She'd got hold of completely the wrong end of the branch and he couldn't really blame her. Not after the dance and the sizzle of awareness that had pervaded the air since they had laid eyes on each other. Even now he sensed an undercurrent of fizz that her anger simply added to. For an instant he felt an almost visceral tug of regret, that by offering Emily a job he was effectively closing the door on any other type of relationship. No matter. The attraction could never have gone anywhere. Emily was Ava's best friend—it was complicated enough between Ava and himself without adding extra mud to the water. Plus, Emily was just out of a messy divorce and therefore she was way too emotionally vulnerable. And Luca would not risk hurting anyone.

'I understand that this seems a little off the wall and I understand why you're suspicious. But this is a genuine job offer with no strings attached. Not a single one.' Different expressions chased across her face, suspicion still held the upper hand, but she didn't move away and he kept talking. 'I love the idea of an advertising campaign on Jalpura. I'd like to make it happen.'

Her brown eyes narrowed. 'That still doesn't explain why you want to use me as the photographer.'

'Because it's your idea and I like the vision you created. You're looking for work—so why not?'

'So it is nothing to do with…?' Heat touched her cheeks but she held his gaze as she gestured towards the dance floor. Closed her eyes, then reopened them. 'Whatever happened out there.'

'What happened out there was due to a mutual attraction. The click factor, if you will. But that now needs to be clicked off. I would never mix business and pleasure, would never offer anyone a job because I expect some sort of sexual quid pro quo.' The idea caused his lips to press together in distaste. 'If we decide to go ahead with a professional relationship, that is exactly what it would be.'

Emily shook her head; her brown eyes held his, searched them. 'So there is no ulterior motive? Is this some sort of pity thing? Because I explained my situation to you. Or did Ava put you up to this?'

'No one put me up to anything.' Yet the question reminded him anew of how close Emily and Ava were and he knew he needed to be wary of that. Especially when it came to Jodi. But that didn't change the fact he wanted Emily for this job. Instinct told him she'd bring the skills he needed, plus now he had this idea he wanted to run with it and, as she herself had said, she was 'ready and available'. And, of course, there was her name, always assuming she'd agree that he could use it.

'It still doesn't make sense. How can you offer me a job without seeing my work? You may hate it.'

It was a fair point. Instinct and convenience were all very well, but… 'You're right. So let's meet tomorrow. Bring your portfolio and we can discuss it. No strings, no commitment. If I decide you aren't suitable for the job or if you decide it's not for you, then we can both walk away. No hard feelings.'

Her fingers drummed on the table and he could see the trouble in her eyes, then she scanned the room and turned to him. 'OK. When and where?'

'Brunch meeting? At Zelda's? It's a bit off the beaten track. I'll ask for a private table.'

'I'll be there.'

The following day Emily approached the agreed upon venue; anticipation vied with anxiety and she glanced down with trepidation at the portfolio she carried. This whole idea was surreal in the extreme; in fact, the more she thought about it, the more her instincts told her this was a bad, bad idea. Too far out of her comfort zone. She wanted a job that she would find easy, preferably working with people she was familiar with.

But what choice did she have? Her networking last night had been an unmitigated disaster.

Phrases filtered back to her. From the indirect *'So sorry, daahling, but I've just put a new team together.'* To the more direct, *'Sorry, Em, but if you will take eighteen months off to play wifey then you can't expect to waltz back in.'*

Incipient panic threatened yet again and before it could take hold she pushed the door of the restaurant open and entered, scanned the occupants and spotted Luca at a large corner table. Holy Moly. Against all odds the man was even hotter in smart casual than he was in a tux. Shower-damp jet-black hair showed a hint of unruly curl, his shirt sleeves rolled up to show tanned muscular forearms that she had a sudden urge to photograph for posterity. Forced herself not to do just that.

He looked up and smiled and she blinked, wishing he didn't have this unsettling effect on her. She didn't like it, didn't want it; it made her feel uncomfortable that she could be so aware of a man. The very idea had seemed impossible a few months ago and somehow it still felt wrong. A near betrayal that she could feel something as primal as desire when for so long all she had felt was the raw ache of grief for her baby, the dull layer of misery blanketing her from all other emotion.

Not now. All too often the slightest thing could trigger a wave of misery, a surge of panic. But somehow she had to suppress it. Forcing a smile to her face, she walked towards Luca as he rose to greet her, saw those silver-grey eyes scan her face. 'Hey.'

'Hey.'

As she sat he pushed the menu towards her, and she looked down, glad of something to do, to distract from the wave of sadness that was about to wash over her. A part of her wanted to succumb, to allow herself to drown in it, to float in the waves and think of all she had lost, all that her baby would never have.

'Are you OK, Emily?' The concern in his deep Italian-tinged voice was palpable and jolted her to the present.

'I'm fine.'

'If this place is not to your liking, we can go somewhere else.'

'No. It's not that.' The restaurant was lovely, vibrant and busy with the hum of people having a weekend brunch. Friends catching up. Families out on a Sunday.

The kind of place she'd always loved but now somehow seemed wrong, seemed designed to show her what she couldn't have. The sight of every baby, every happy family an emphasis of what she'd lost before she even had it. Did a career even matter compared to the precious life she'd lost? Because deep down she knew it was her own fault. She should have taken more care, not been so blithely confident. She shouldn't have let Howard bully her into hiding her pregnancy, shouldn't have been so intent on trying to make him happy, shouldn't have attended parties, dressed to the nines, in high heels to try and disguise her pregnancy. The sense that she'd somehow jinxed her pregnancy was irrational but unshakeable.

'Emily?' Luca's voice recalled her to the present, reminded her to get a grip. Her career might no longer feel relevant but she needed a job. And she would not let her own personal situation impact on her professionalism any more. If she did this job she would give it her best, however tarnished that might be. 'This is perfect. Truly. I'll have the pancakes. With bacon and maple syrup.'

'Good choice.'

A waitress came and took their order and soon reappeared with their drinks.

Emily sipped the foam of her cappuccino and said, 'So…how would you like to do this?'

'Would you like to show me your portfolio first?'

'Sure.' The idea of displaying her work filled her with a sudden sharp surge of dread, and frustration filled her. What was wrong with her? Two years ago she'd been an up-and-coming fashion photographer. The stuff in her portfolio was excellent and she knew it. Or at least she had known it once, before Howard's ongoing critiques had dulled the gloss of her pictures, distorted the way she saw her work. Picking up the slim folder, she handed it across the table, tried not to let her gaze linger on the strong shape of his hand, the deft, competent grip of his fingers. Photographer's eye, she told herself. Or an overreaction due to nerves. 'I've brought a small printed portfolio and I'll show you a digital gallery as well.'

As he opened the leather-bound binder, she couldn't watch, almost didn't want to see his reaction, busied herself with booting up her netbook.

Finally she knew she couldn't stare at the screen any more so she looked up and across at him. Saw the binder still open, though his gaze was now on her.

'Obviously, as I said, I am a fashion photographer, so my portfolio mostly consists of examples of fashion photography. I did include a couple of still-life pictures I did for a National Trust campaign. But I do think you should consider taking on someone with more experience of commercial photography.'

What? What are you doing, Emily? Talking yourself out of the job? Pressing her lips together, she focused on not talking. At all.

'I appreciate your honesty and I get it's a risk but it's one I'm willing to take.' And again Emily wondered what was going on, why he was so set on employing her without even considering anyone else. She was sure it wasn't anything to do with the latent smoulder of attraction that had sparked the previous night; she'd believed his assertion that he would never mix business and pleasure. Yet instinct, finely honed instinct, still warned her there was something else. Some reason he wanted to move so fast.

'Why? Why would you take that risk?'

'Your photos show vibrancy and flair and originality. I love how you use shape and colour and background effect. Plus the two different pictures of Ava showcase how you can use the same model to portray completely different things.'

The sincerity in his voice was evident and relief swathed her; the job wasn't a sinecure. He'd studied the pictures and grasped what she'd tried to do and he liked it. The knowledge sparked a small, unfamiliar surge of confidence. 'Ava was a great model to work with.'

'Yes. But the idea, the lighting, the captured image is down to you. In the perfume ad you have conveyed the essence of flowers and lightness in a way that's difficult to explain—but it works.'

Emily frowned; she had been particularly proud of that photograph, yet it was one that Howard had targeted as frivolous and dismissed as cutesy. And she'd accepted that criticism as just, but now, as she looked at it again, her frown deepened.

'I would like to know how you did it.'

'The original plan was to have Ava sitting in a meadow of flowers with the sun shining down on her, but that seemed a little too clichéd. So I persuaded the director to give my idea a go. To be subtler.' She'd kept it simple, Ava bathed in the light of a setting sun, wearing a floaty summery dress, a circlet of flowers in her hair and a daisy chain around her wrist. Looking almost ethereal.

As she spoke she remembered the person she had been then: a woman confident in herself and her ideas, happy to offer her thoughts and opinions. A woman who'd believed in herself. Where had that Emily gone? Right now she truly didn't know. Somewhere along the way her faith in herself had seeped away—but as she studied the photo, listened to Luca's words, she could feel a small trickle of pride.

He nodded. 'It worked. Perfectly. And it encapsulates what I want for my campaign. Something that captures the essence of my chocolate and where it comes from. You somehow made the viewer want to smell like the perfume. I need you to make the viewer want to taste my chocolate. Can you do it?'

The questions preceded the arrival of their food and as the waiter busied himself with serving their pancakes and refilling the coffees it gave her time to think. As she did so her mind began to play with ideas, a familiar spark that she hadn't felt for a long time. Brought on by having her work valued. By someone uninfluenced by Howard or by past association of any sort.

And so, once the waiter had left, she leant forward and said, 'I don't know if I can do it and that's the truth. But I'd like to try.' She picked up her knife and fork. 'Let me see if I can come up with an idea.'

'Is there anything I can do to help?'

Emily took a mouthful of pancake as she considered. 'I need more information.' She glanced at him. 'I know this may sound nuts but I need to know about Palazzo di Cioccolato, about your company ethos, about all your chocolate and, of course, as much as possible about this particular chocolate. When I did this ad I spoke to the perfumier who created it. I knew absolutely everything there was to know about that perfume. The circlet of flowers in Ava's hair was made up of the flowers in the scent itself. But I also wore the perfume myself, spoke to people who wore it. Got my friends to wear it...'

There was a silence and she wondered if she'd blown it. 'Sorry. There was no need for you to know any of that. Give me a few days and I'll get back to you with an idea.'

'No need to apologise. I like your enthusiasm.' His voice was deep and there was something in his silver-grey eyes, a warmth that heated up her insides, a balm to her soul lacerated by Howard's put-downs. 'And it obviously gets results. So I am happy to provide you with as much company information as you need. How about I start with an overview? In terms of ethos I always try to use the best ingredients possible—no hidden rubbish. I want my product to be affordable, but I won't compete with supersize mass-produced products. I know it is possible to buy a huge bar of chocolate for a low cost. I'd prefer people to choose to spend the same amount for a smaller bar because it's worth it. I see chocolate as something to be savoured, a luxury, a treat that is worth looking forward to, spending time on.'

His words held a depth and a tone that seemed to epitomise the chocolate itself, and Emily was sucked in by the words, and his sheer charisma, the delicious sexiness of a man speaking of chocolate with such appreciation. She cleared her throat. 'Sounds good. What about the new range?'

'I want this to be a little different, an experiment with fruit and spices. I want it to feel decadent and new. I've spent the past year tasting, mixing, thinking, tasting again, sourcing… I am hoping this will be a major player in the premium chocolate market.'

Decadent and new…the deep rumble of those words sent a sudden rush over her skin, the animation in his voice, the fact that he got so involved. Her gaze lingered on his hands as she pictured him intent over the recipe, stirring, tasting, and now her eyes moved to his lips and she pictured him tasting the chocolate. Jeez. Get a grip. Think.

'That's all great,' she managed. 'That gives me a real feel for what you represent.'

'Good. So what do you think about the project? Are you interested?'

The questions seemed to take on too much meaning.

Her gaze kept returning to the lithe muscle of his forearm, the way his shirt glided over the breadth of his chest, the allure of his eyes, the jut of a nose that proclaimed both confidence and arrogance. But it was also his aura—there was something powerful and scary about his air of contained energy, the feeling that he was a man on a mission, a man who would carry out his agenda whatever that might be. A man who most likely didn't suffer fools gladly, and a momentary doubt struck her. She questioned whether she had the strength to take that on, risk being assessed and found wanting. Again.

Throughout her marriage with Howard she had tried so hard to win his praise for her work, had wanted so much to prove she had the talent to move into a different sphere of photography. To no avail—in the end she'd had to accept she simply wasn't good enough, and somehow that had transcended so her belief in herself had been diminished. And now the pressure to succeed, to fulfil Luca's unexpected belief in her, felt almost too much. Almost.

Because she would not give in, would not return to the despair of the past months, despite the temptation, the enticement of cocooning herself from the world because it made her feel closer to her baby.

Not happening, because the world had intruded in its reality, the ping of unpaid bills arriving in her inbox. She needed a job—the alternative would be to turn to her parents for help. The idea was unacceptable.

Perhaps they would help, but they hadn't thought to offer. Had given her practically no emotional support throughout the past months. For her mother infidelity and divorce, smashed dreams and the failure of love were the norm. As for the miscarriage, for Marigold, a woman who had never wanted a family, she simply didn't get it. She had tried—descended on the flat with expensive gifts, wine, chocolate and flowers—and in truth Emily had appreciated the gesture, accepted it was the best her mother could do. Her father had called her a couple of times, expressed his sympathy, the conversation full of encouragement about how he knew Emily would move on. 'Other fish in the sea.' 'So many women have a miscarriage and go on to have many children.' And Emily had concurred—knew that her father too was doing his best. But then, duty done, her parents had both gone back to their normal lives.

And that was the point: she was peripheral to their lives, and as such her independence was a matter of pride to her. She would never ask for anything, just accept what they could give.

So now, she met Luca's gaze and nodded. 'Yes. I'm interested.'

'Excellent.' He sipped his coffee, drummed his fingers on the table top. 'I've got an idea.'

Emily glanced at him, wondered if she could deal with any more of Luca's ideas, sensed that this one would be another humdinger. 'What's that?' she asked as trepidation prickled her spine.

CHAPTER FOUR

LUCA DID ONE last quick recap of the pros and cons and then, 'It's a way for you to learn more about Palazzo di Cioccolato. Come back to Turin with me tomorrow and I'll give you a tour of the factory and headquarters. I really like the way you immerse yourself in everything to do with the product and I think the best way to get a real feel for the business is to see it for yourself.'

Emily put her coffee cup down with a sudden *thunk*. 'Tomorrow?'

'Why not?' Now he had a plan, he *wanted* to move fast, wanted to find his sister. Because whilst Jodi was a grown woman, and more than capable of looking after herself...he was her big brother and part of his job, his role in life, was to look after her. Ever since his father had walked out Luca had vowed, sworn to himself, that he would be the man of the family. And when, seven months after his dad had gone, Jodi had been born, a deep, deep protectiveness had come over him. A sense of responsibility so profound he could still remember the weight of the mantle he'd gladly accepted. So right now he couldn't see any reason to wait. 'My idea is we spend a couple of days in Italy and then head straight to Jalpura from there.'

Now Emily stared at him, her brown eyes wide, and he suspected she was evaluating his sanity levels. 'Whoa. Hang on a minute. How exactly is this going to work?' Emily raised her hands in a gesture that conveyed bafflement and he couldn't help but note the fluid grace of her movements. His gaze lingered on the elegant shape of her fingers, the supple delicacy of her wrists. *Focus, Luca.* 'Do you know how an ad campaign works?'

'Of course, I do.' He shrugged. 'Well, maybe not the detail. I have an agency that usually deals with that.'

'Well, I am not an expert, but I do know how to do a photo shoot. Usually I work with a production company. You need to do a massive amount of research, decide on the campaign and how it would work. We need to find a location, a model or more than one model. Once we find that we need to figure out clothing, we need a stylist, a make-up artist, someone to make the location look right, a lighting expert. I can't just go to Jalpura and pluck a person out of thin air, hand them a bar of chocolate and take a photo.'

'I get that.' And he did—realised he hadn't fully thought this through. 'This trip to Jalpura would be preliminary, a research trip, to give you some ideas.'

Her eyes narrowed. 'Why do I get the feeling you made all that up on the spot?'

'Does it matter if I did? I want to run with this.'

'Enough that you want to drop everything to research an ad campaign yourself that you only thought of yesterday.'

'Yes. There is no point in wasting time once a decision is made.'

'But why? Surely you have a marketing director or someone else who would usually do this.'

'I do. But I'm also a hands-on CEO. I work across all departments. I do stints in packaging, delivery, tasting, everything. Otherwise I think it's too easy to get distanced from reality. I want to produce chocolate for everyone and for me to do that I need to understand every facet of my business. I don't want to end up consumed only by admin and spreadsheets and profit margins.' All true. 'This feels right—I want to get it done. Yes, obviously, I have some stuff scheduled but I have a very efficient team of people and I can manage to be away for a few days.' He paused.

'Though we'll need to sort out a visa for you. Mine is still valid from my last visit.'

'I have a valid visa already. I got a five-year one that hasn't run out as yet.' He could hear reluctance in the admission.

'So how does this sound? We head to Turin tomorrow afternoon. Next day the factory tour, after that we fly to Jalpura. Stay there a few days and we'll be back in a week.'

'A week?' There was a small catch in her voice, her brown eyes wide with doubt, her upper lip caught in her teeth. His eyes lingered and caught on her mouth, before he wrenched his gaze away, stared into the dregs of his espresso and tried to dismiss a sudden niggle of doubt. A week with Emily. Seven days, seven nights… With a woman who impacted him in a way he didn't understand.

His glib words of the previous night mocked him. *Instant connection, mutual attraction, click factor.* It was all that and more.

Resolutely he stopped the thoughts in their tracks. The die was cast and once this had become professional the attraction factor was irrelevant.

'A week,' he repeated firmly. 'That should be enough.'

More than enough. He wasn't sure if she'd actually said the words or he'd imagined them.

'OK.' She nodded and he sensed she was trying to convince herself. 'It's not as though we will be spending every minute together. I'll get on with my own thing; I don't need hand-holding.'

His gaze dropped to study her hands, the slender length, the short unpainted nails, the faint line where her wedding ring had once been. *Stop looking.* But as he wrenched his eyes away he saw that Emily's gaze loitered on *his* hands, her eyes wide. She pressed her lips together as if to moisten them and desire gave a fierce tug in his gut.

Sufficientemente. Enough, Petrovelli. Professional, remember?

'Excellent, as I don't plan to hold your hand.' The words were too harsh and he did his best to smile. 'Because you won't need me to—I trust you to get on with it. So, do we have a deal? I propose to pay you a flat fee of five thousand pounds for this week and all expenses paid. After that you can invoice me for the hours you put in.'

A silence and he'd give a lot to know what was going through her head. Then she nodded. 'That sounds more than fair. We have a deal.'

Relief mixed with satisfaction—Mission Jalpura was on. Which meant perhaps now was a good time to tell Emily about Jodi, ask her if she would be willing to use her name to help him in his search. But the words wouldn't come; instead an image of his sister filled his mind. Dark curls, fierce-eyed. And the words of their last conversation.

'Please, Luca, let it be. I am OK, I just need to figure some stuff out and to do that I need space and time.'

'But—'

'No buts, Luca. This is my business, not yours. I appreciate your concern, but please leave it be. No big-brother stuff. My business, OK? Got it?'

Her lips had turned up in a smile as she'd said the words, but the underlay of seriousness had been clear.

It was Jodi's business and he'd done his best to stand by his sister's request. Had held back, done nothing, but now he couldn't do that any more, not when he sensed there was something wrong, that Jodi needed help. And this opportunity to take action had come along. But if Jodi didn't want to confide in Luca or Therese, she'd definitely recoil at the thought of Emily knowing anything. In which case he owed it to Jodi to try and find the answers on his own; he'd bring Emily in only if he needed to. So there was no need to tell her anything now. For a second discomfort edged him and he dismissed it. He'd tell Emily if and only if it became necessary; in the meantime, he was employing her to do a genuine job.

'Great. I'll get a contract drawn up.'

She held her hand out and he hesitated, told himself not to be an idiot. What did he think would happen if he shook her hand? He'd combust? His hand would light up? He reached out and took her hand in his, resisted the urge to instantly drop it. Because the simple touch did affect him, pulled back the memory of their dance yesterday, enough to conjure desire right back up.

Dropping her hand, he cleared his throat. 'Right. I'll try and get you on the same flight.' He pulled his phone out of his pocket and a few minutes later nodded. 'As luck would have it there is a seat free. We can travel together. Can you meet me in the first-class lounge tomorrow afternoon?'

'I'll be there.' Emily's voice seemed taut and, in all truth, Luca couldn't blame her.

Emily walked through the busy airport lounge, pulling her suitcase behind her, gripping the handle so hard it hurt as she battled the sense of surreal. Until now she'd focused on packing, on getting here on time, but, now that she had made it, as she approached the meeting point her nerves fluttered and she tightened her muscles to counteract them, felt the insidious flick of panic.

She braced herself against the fear that she *couldn't* do this job. Somehow when she'd been with Luca it had all seemed possible. The ideas had buzzed, caught up in his own clear enthusiasm for the project and his equally clear strength of feeling for the product and for his company. This man would expect the best, deserved the best, and now all of Howard's jibes rang and danced in her brain, told her she'd bitten off more than she could chew.

Emily gritted her teeth. This was the only job on offer. Striding forward, she raised an arm in greeting, forced herself to project a confidence she didn't even feel a flicker of.

'Hey.'

'Hey.'

'Shall we head to the departure lounge? We've time to grab a coffee before boarding.'

'Sure.' But she could feel her steps lag as they started to walk, as the flutter of nerves turned into a pirouette. For the past months she had spent nigh on every waking and sleeping minute in the sanctuary of her home. Now here she was about to embark on a global trip. And now the panic began to build, to twist and layer itself into knots of tension that tangled inside her.

She tried to focus, found her gaze riveted to

Luca and decided to give in and be shallow in the hope his sheer aura would exert a soothing calm. So as they walked she studied him as she would a model, the jut of his jaw, the swell of his biceps and the tantalising strength he exuded. The kind of strength that would blanket and cocoon you in safety. And, politically correct or not, that carried her through the process of boarding, finding their seats and getting settled. Allowed her to try and suppress the growing, escalating swoosh and whoosh and pound of irrational dread.

Until the flight actually took off and the anxiety whirled in her head, turned and twisted her stomach in a nauseating spin. Closing her eyes, she concentrated on her breathing, on slowing her pulse rate.

'You OK?' Luca turned to her and she tried to speak, her hands gripping the arm rest as she forced her vocal cords to work.

'Fine.' The syllable sounded strangled but she hoped it would be enough.

'Hey. It's OK.' His deep voice held concern but also a calm reassurance that at least didn't escalate the numbing fear that had sent her fight-or-flight response into deadlock. 'I'm guessing you have a fear of flying.'

It was a fair assumption but not true; this was a panic attack, brought on by the inescapable knowledge that she was heading away from the sanctuary of home, coalesced with the sudden realisation and guilt that she had taken this first step to moving on with life. All she wanted was to go back home, to the almost comfort of the abyss of despair that kept her close to her lost baby. What was she doing? How could she move on from him, the being whom she had loved so much?

None of this was anything she could or would share with Luca, even if she could speak, which right now she couldn't. All her effort was concentrated on staying put, and not running up and down the plane in an attempt to get out.

He continued to speak, his tone soothing and almost conversational. 'Jodi used to be terrified on planes—she'd hold my hand as tight as she could during take-off. She said it helped, stopped her from running to the pilot and begging him to take the plane down. We can try that, if you like.'

And so she gripped his hand, with all her might, focused on the cool reassuring strength of his grasp, the scope of his palm, the feel of his fingers encircling hers, closed her eyes and tried to think soothing thoughts. Time seemed to slow and ebb, but slowly the wave of panic stemmed and then subsided, as if his touch somehow soothed the tangle of chaos inside. Unknotted her insides and now, instead of panic, a different sensation pervaded with a gooey warmth, invaded her veins with a liquid heat. Now his hold encircled her with awareness, charged her with desire and she released him as tell-tale heat flushed her cheeks.

A sideways glance revealed an expression of shock flitting across his face as he looked down at his hand and she wondered if he'd felt something too.

Quickly she burst into speech. 'Well, that was embarrassing. Especially when I said I didn't need hand-holding.' She tried a smile, hoped it didn't wobble too much and he smiled back, the smile full wattage, and it curled her toes.

'Don't worry about it. Truly. How are you feeling now?'

'A lot better. Thank you—I didn't hurt you, did I?' She studied his hand and again a frisson ran through her; his fingers combined strength with a masculine beauty that fascinated her, the breadth of his palm, the compact sturdiness of his wrist. This had to stop. All she could think was that this was some sort of aftershock, a reaction to her panic, but her awareness of the man next to her had grown exponentially.

Her gaze roved upwards; she saw the shape of his tanned forearm, the curve of his biceps, the width of his shoulder. Continued to take in his face, the angle of his cheekbone, the jut of his determined jaw and now her eyes lingered on the shape of his mouth.

Oh, God. As she forced herself to meet his gaze she saw something in his expression, a spark, and she sensed he had clocked and understood her scrutiny.

'No. You did not hurt me at all. Please feel free to make use of my hand again.' The deep undertone had a layer of suggestion, just the smallest hint of a double entendre, and she looked at him with a small question of wonder. Had she imagined it?

'Thank you. But I think I'll be OK.'

'Do you often suffer from a fear of flying?'

'No.' Realising the abruptness of the answer, Emily wished she had simply claimed that as the reason. 'This is the first time so hopefully it's a one-off. Plus, the prospect of seeing Turin cancels any panic.'

For a moment she thought he'd pursue the topic but instead he clearly decided to accept her disinclination to discuss the issue further. 'Have you been to Turin before?'

'No, but I am looking forward to it. I haven't had a chance to do a lot of research, but I do know that it is meant to be an amazing place. Full of history and tradition.'

'It is. Turin has a real sense of tradition and

the past. It is also, of course, the capital of chocolate. The very first chocolate bar originated in Turin. And in 1678 the Queen of Savoy granted a chocolate maker from Turin a licence to open the first chocolate house, so like a tea or coffee house today. And today the Piedmont region produces about eighty-five thousand tons of chocolate a year.' He came to a stop. 'Listen to me. I sound like a tour guide.'

Emily shook her head. 'You sound like someone who is very proud of their city. A city that sounds like chocolate heaven. I'll make sure I make time to look round, get some photos. I can see that Turin itself is important to the essence of your chocolate and I think we need to get that idea in somehow, even though we will be shooting in Jalpura.'

He hesitated. 'If you would like I could take you around Turin, if that would help.'

A thrill of anticipation shot through her, one she quelled instantly. This was work related, nothing more. 'That would be wonderful, and it will really help to see Turin through your eyes.'

'Then I'd be happy to be your guide. We can start tonight. I'll pick you up from your hotel at seven.'

'Perfect. Thank you.' There was that sense of looking forward. Again. And she hadn't even noticed that the plane had begun its descent.

CHAPTER FIVE

EMILY GLANCED AT her watch: five minutes to seven. She surveyed her reflection in the hotel mirror, reminded herself she was done with dressing for a man. Any man. Before Howard she'd never dressed to be noticed, had preferred to blend into whatever scenario she found herself. Knew that as a photographer it made sense to be as invisible as possible and Emily was good at that. Invisibility was her watchword. Much of her childhood had been spent relegating herself to the background, tiptoeing around her mother and the man de jour. As she'd got older she'd disliked being feted because of her famous parents. So she'd learnt to dress to not be noticed.

Until Howard. Once she'd met him somehow she'd ended up dressing to please him.

'How you look reflects on me. I need you to be beautiful, elegant, poised and attractive...'

'Emily, sweetie, of course I love you for you,

but I am a photographer—I need to be surrounded by beauty and I have an image to uphold. My wife cannot be a dowd.'

And somehow Howard had started to dictate her wardrobe and from there it had descended into snide criticisms and put-downs if she had so much as a hair out of place. Worse perhaps had been his habit of studying her and then emitting a small frustrated sigh, a shake of his head and then, 'Honestly, Em. Why can't you ever get it right?'

Never again would she dress for a man, so she should be happy with her appearance tonight. Smart casual black trousers and a plain demure button-up blouse with a collar, complemented by a pair of boring but serviceable, smart black pumps. Hair pulled up into a businesslike bun. Professional, boring and invisible. Perfect.

So why did she look so glum? Why was she wishing she'd packed a dress from the Howard era? Why was her hand hovering over her make-up? Why did her fingers itch to pull her hair loose?

The answer was obvious—dark haired, gorgeous, as sinful as the chocolate he created, Luca Petrovelli. Which was ridiculous. But something had happened on the plane—perhaps it was his instinctive ability to ward off her panic without belittling it as Howard would have. Or his clear enthusiasm and love for his home city. Or perhaps it was the thought of a night out, a chance to see a city she'd never seen, guided by a man who had succeeded in waking her hormones from a sleep she'd believed to be permanent.

Whatever it was it was time to go; one last glance in the mirror and she headed for the door. Reminded herself that this was a business meeting, a chance for her to work out how to incorporate elements of Turin into the ad campaign. And get to know the founder of Palazzo di Cioccolato better.

She scooped up a lightweight jacket and headed out of the elegant hotel room. As she entered the marble lobby she saw Luca by the front desk and her heart skipped a beat. He looked positively scrumptious—black hair, shower-damp and spiky. Shirt and chinos and a jacket hooked on one finger over his shoulder—he could have stepped out of a glossy magazine. In fact her fingers itched to capture the image. Itched to do way more than that—the tantalising V of his chest made her head spin and she forced her feet to maintain a steady pace towards him. Even as she fought the urge to race past him, find a boutique, buy a dress and transform herself.

Really, Emily? Shallow, much.

'Buonasera.' The timbre of his voice washed

over her as he smiled at her. 'I hope the hotel is OK?'

'It's wonderful. The room is beautiful and it's got a marvellous view of Turin.'

'Good. I plan to show you the sights a little more personally. I thought we could walk the streets for a little, then I will take you to Silvio's, a cocktail bar where I used to work. They do the best cocktails in Turin and the food is pretty good too.'

'That sounds lovely.' She couldn't remember the last time she'd gone out for cocktails and dinner and the idea filled her with an unbidden sense of excitement. 'So tell me about your cocktail-shaking skills.'

'I am a pro. I can make a martini shaken or stirred. I invented at least three pretty brilliant mixes. Silvio still serves them today.' Emily suspected that whatever Luca turned his mind to he would be the best at, the knowledge both potent and ever so slightly intimidating. After all, Howard had been excellent at what he'd done and it had made him both arrogant and cranky. *Stop.* Tonight she didn't want her ex-husband to intrude—instead she wanted to try to enjoy this evening. The idea was a novel one, brought about by being in a new place, the scent of Italy…the buzz of a different language around her.

As they stepped out into the balmy air Emily inhaled. 'I love the smell of Italy.' Though truth be told she'd swear she could also catch Luca's scent, a crisp, deep note of bergamot and citrus that added to the sudden heady feeling. This unfurling of enjoyment had been absent for too long and she suspected it would be a short-lived burst before the shadows set back in. For a moment the rawness of grief and loss cast a darkness; it shouldn't be like this. She should be home, with her baby, celebrating the milestones: a first tooth, a smile...all things her baby hadn't had the chance to experience. *Not now.* Instead she pulled in air, refocused on the smell and the sights around her, allowed them to create a bubble that insulated her from the might-have-beens.

Luca's gaze rested on her face and she saw the dawn of concern and knew she must head it off. 'I can smell garlic and oregano and chocolate.'

'My chocolate in particular, of course.'

'Of course.' She returned his smile. 'It must feel amazing to be part of Turin's history. Part of how chocolate has evolved through the years.'

He looked struck. 'I'm not sure I ever thought about it like that. Thank you.' His smile was genuine and he looked absurdly youthful and it touched her even as she wondered how he did see himself.

Absurd shyness overcame her and she took refuge in what she knew best. 'Would you mind if I take pictures as we walk?' The camera was her equivalent of a safety blanket.

'Of course.'

As they walked she looked round, snapped away, took in the wide tree-lined boulevards, the buildings of varying sizes and shapes that oozed history and colour. Elegant gardens vied for attention with a proliferation of formal beds that looked centuries old.

Luca seemed content to walk beside her, occasionally pointing out a place of interest.

Until, 'We're here. This is Silvio's.' Emily gazed around at the square, absorbed the sheer feel of the history of the buildings, shops and cafés. In the middle was a church, an architectural mix of bell tower, walls, domes and a neo-classical face that combined to create an awe-inspiring awareness of how long people had worshipped here.

Following her gaze, Luca said, 'This is one of Turin's most loved places of worship; it has been added to over the centuries and is said to be a place of healing.'

'It's beautiful,' Emily said softly. 'It all is.'

Luca nodded towards a small café. 'That has been there since the mid-seventeen-hundreds.

We should come here tomorrow for a cup of *bicerin*.'

'I'd like that. Layers of espresso, chocolate and milk, right?'

'Right.'

She smiled at him. 'It's a date.' The words seemed to echo softly round the square and she hastened to clarify. 'Not a real date, obviously. Just a business date.'

'Of course.' His voice was smooth but laced with amusement and she felt heat flush her face. 'Shall we go in?'

Luca looked round the familiar, eclectic interior of the bar he had worked in for years. The walls were a vibrant blue, and empty bottles were suspended from the ceiling in an eye watering zig-zag display. Small mosaic-topped tables were scattered over the wooden floor, the air hummed with conversation, and the scents of fruit and food and a sheer vibrancy that always gave him a buzz.

'Luca.' The waist-coated man moved from behind the bar arms outstretched and Luca moved forward, clasped hands and exchanged a hug before turning to Emily.

'Emily, this is Matteo, my old manager.'

'Your old boss,' the Italian corrected with a beaming smile.

'Matteo, this is Emily Khatri, a business colleague, here to get some photographic inspiration on Turin.'

'Enchanted to meet you.' Luca saw the appreciation in his old friend's eyes as they rested on Emily and felt a sudden absurd stab of emotion. Whoa. What was that? Jealousy? That was both irrational and ridiculous. Emily was not the type of woman he would enter into a relationship with; she was just out of a relationship, she was clearly vulnerable, she had got married, which implied she believed in the fallacy of love and, as icing on the proverbial panettone, she was Ava's best friend. In other words, he had no claim on her whatsoever, yet a stab of irritation jabbed him as Matteo smiled at Emily and engaged her in a flirtatious conversation.

Luca gave his head a small shake. He knew exactly how negative an emotion jealousy was—it had been the downfall of his first relationship. He had been so terrified Lydia would leave him he had smothered her in love, hated it when she so much as looked at another man. Ironically enough, in the end, she had left him for another man. A rich, handsome, charming man who 'knew how to have fun'. Just as his father had left him for a rich, aristocratic woman who had financed his path to success. The parallels were impossible to ignore and he'd learnt a lesson he would never forget. Do not get involved; if you don't feel love, you can't fear its loss, can't let that fear generate negative emotions, take over your every waking moment with dread of the inevitable. Even better, you couldn't experience the pain of loss when the inevitable happened. As it inescapably would.

Never again. And in truth, since Lydia, no woman had ignited so much as the smallest spark of jealousy—he'd always been in control of his liaisons. Luca shook his head. Jealousy was a mire of negativity that would have no place at his table. Certainly not now. Matteo was one of his dearest friends. And Emily was a business colleague. And if for some inexplicable reason attraction was distorting into feelings of jealousy it was time to rein the attraction in. Fast.

They were both looking at him. 'Is all well, Luca?' Matteo asked and he'd swear he saw a smile lurk in his friend's eyes.

'Yes. Sorry.' He pulled a smile to his face. 'I was daydreaming about my many hours behind the bar.' Now he turned to Emily. 'Have you chosen a cocktail?'

'Not yet. I was going to see if I could have one of your signature ones.'

'Better yet,' Matteo said. 'Why don't you mix it, Luca? Show Emily how it is done. You are both welcome behind the bar. In the meantime, I had better serve some customers.' He waved a hand to one of the other staff. 'Keep a table for Luca.' He smiled at Emily. 'It will be good, I promise. Luca was the best in the business.'

As Matteo moved away Luca knew how foolish he'd been. Presumably the misplaced jealousy was simply another symptom of his current emotional state—a state he *would* supress. As he would suppress this attraction. Yet he sensed perspiration form on the back of his neck as he eyed the somewhat small space behind the bar. Forcing his jaw to unclench, he managed a smile as he gestured to the area. 'Come, I will show you how to make *martini cioccolato di Luca.*'

'Luca's chocolate martini?' she asked, with the faintest gurgle of laughter.

'It sounds better in Italian,' he conceded. 'Try it.'

She repeated the Italian words and then grimaced. 'I sound ridiculous. I have no aptitude for language.'

'You need to say it with more emphasis, make each syllable more dramatic, more passionate. *Martini cioccolaaato.*' His over-emphasis brought a smile to her face and he felt ridiculously pleased. 'You have a go.'

'*Martini cioccolaaato.*' She stopped and gave a small delicious chuckle. 'Like that?'

'Excellent. Now come, let us get started.' He paused. 'As long as you are sure you would like this particular cocktail. It is a little decadent—a bit like having dessert before your main course.'

'I can do that,' she said. 'In fact, I'd like to do that.'

'Sometimes it is good to do something a little bit sinful.' The words fell from his lips without intent, as if his vocal cords had been taken hostage. Created a shimmer of awareness, carried on the waves of noise and chatter and the clink of glass.

'Then let's get started.' Her words were low as her breath caught.

He led the way behind the bar, to a secluded corner, and now he was, oh, so aware of her proximity, the scent of her vanilla shampoo, and a subtle refreshing hint of her perfume. *Keep it together.* 'Have you ever shaken a cocktail before?'

Emily shook her head. 'Nope. And I feel I should warn you now that my culinary skills are not particularly good.'

'No worries. I'll run over the basics. Then just copy what I do.'

He was aware of her studying him as he set out the ingredients, suspected she wanted to take photos. 'So we have vodka, we have a *bicerin* chocolate liqueur, we have an espresso and we have my secret ingredient.' He picked up a grapefruit. 'This adds a sour kick to counteract the sweetness of the chocolate and the darkness of the coffee.' Quickly he cut the grapefruit in half and juiced it.

'That sounds divine. So what now? We put all the ingredients in with some ice and shake?'

Luca couldn't keep the pained expression from his face and Emily gave another gurgle of laughter. 'Sorry. I am guessing that's like someone saying to me "so I just point and click"?'

'Exactly. Mixing a cocktail is an art. You need the measure of ingredients to be exactly right, the perfect combination of strength and sweetness, depth and light.' As he spoke he was aware of her gaze on him, the widening eyes, felt his own pulse ratchet up a notch at the undertones of his words. 'Sometimes you need a cocktail with a bit of spice, like a chilli, or other days you may feel like something a little more bland, but with a kick, like a vanilla martini. Different moods call for a different touch. But the most important thing is to get the balance right.'

Her breathing quickened and heat flushed the angles of her cheekbones to a red-brown glow. 'It sounds almost Zen-like.'

'And the art of the Zen master is to make

sure every cocktail, whatever the mix, brings satisfaction.'

Their gazes locked and the surroundings no longer mattered, the voices on mute, the blue of the walls seeming to fade as his lips tingled with the urge to kiss her, to lean forward and taste her lips.

The spell was broken by the bartender, who stepped in and reached up for a bottle of spirits. 'Sorry, mate,' he said, in a cheerful London twang. 'I need the spiced rum.'

'No problem.'

They spoke simultaneously and Emily took a small step backward.

'Right,' Luca said, knowing he had to use words to bridge the awkwardness. 'So, we need to very carefully measure each ingredient.' Relief touched her expression as she concentrated on the amounts and he continued to speak. 'So this is a two-piece shaker. It's made of stainless steel, which I think is better than glass. It creates a purer cocktail. You put the ingredients in the smaller cup. And now we need the ice. I use ice straight from the freezer to reduce any possible dilution factor. The ice goes in the top half.' Her forehead creased in a small frown of concentration, he saw a glimpse of her teeth as she bit into her upper lip, her whole body taut as she copied his actions, and desire tugged inside him again. 'So now we get ready to shake. Tip the top half over the smaller one as quick as you can so you don't spill any ice.'

She hesitated and he saw doubt cross her face. 'What if I miss?'

'Then we start again. It's no big deal.' Yet it seemed as if to Emily it was. 'Hey, no one is expecting you to be perfect. Honestly, when I started I made at least a million mistakes. But I think you've got this.'

She raised an eyebrow but he saw a hint of a smile. 'Somehow I doubt that, but thank you for making me feel better. Here goes.' In one fluid movement she did as he'd said.

'Perfect. Now tap the top to form a seal and you're ready to shake.'

Now a smile did tip her lips and he could tell the success had given her a small thrill of satisfaction. 'So are there any special moves?'

'Of course.' He walked over to the music section and chose a track. 'Caribbean drum beat for twelve seconds. Ready, set, go.'

He started to shake, keeping the rhythm of the drums. For a moment she stood as if mesmerised and then followed suit, closed her eyes and he allowed himself to watch, the sway of her body, the entranced look on her face as if she were lost in the movement. And he sensed this was an instant of escape, wondered what she was escaping from. 'Now we strain it and then we're done.'

A few minutes later Emily surveyed the two glasses, tipped her head to one side. 'They look beautiful,' she proclaimed and, no surprise, she pulled out her phone and took a picture. 'Now how about we taste them?'

He led the way to the small square table in the corner and placed his drink down on the mosaic top, moved round to pull her chair out before sitting down. 'Cheers,' he said and she raised her glass, full of the dark rich liquid. Carefully she tasted it and closed her eyes in sheer delight. 'It's incredible. I can taste the hint of grapefruit but it's not overpowering, just the teensiest bit astringent.' She took another sip. 'The world of chocolate may have benefited but the land of cocktails definitely missed out.'

She smiled as a waiter approached and her eyes widened as a wooden platter was placed on the table between them. Cold cuts of salami and thin slices of Parma ham, bowls of plump olives, sliced rustic bread, cheeses, were all laid out beautifully.

'This is incredible. I hadn't even realised how hungry I was until I saw this.'

'Usually this would be a pre-dinner snack. *Aperitivo* originated years ago when a man in Turin invented vermouth. He claimed it was a good thing to drink pre-dinner. Then it all evolved and now all over Italy people have pre-dinner drinks and snacks and most bars serve something. Today I asked Matteo for enough for a meal.'

'No wonder you love this city,' Emily said as she picked up a piece of bread. 'When did you move here?'

'When I was eleven.' A shadow crossed his face as he recalled the reason for the relocation from England. For the previous six months his life had been made a living hell by a gang of schoolyard bullies. The daily rituals of taunts and humiliations, pain and misery still occasionally populated his dreams. Worst of all had been his anger at his own weakness, the soul-churning knowledge that he couldn't stand up for himself. A weakness he had refused to reveal to anyone.

But eventually the situation had escalated and his mother, once alerted to the problem, had gone into characteristic action. Had changed their name to her maiden name of Petrovelli and whisked the family to Italy to live, away from England where Dolci and the new Casseveti family continued to flourish. 'Mum said it was a new start. She got a job here and we never looked back.' The words sounded hollow even as he said them; in truth you could argue he had spent his whole life looking back.

As if she sensed the demon on his back she reached out and placed her hand over his. The warmth of her touch, the sense of her fingers shivered a small shock through him. 'It's hard not to look back,' she said gently. 'And there is nothing wrong with looking back, staying close to the past. There are some things we should never forget.'

And he saw such sadness in her eyes that pain touched his chest and he covered her hand, so it was sandwiched between his. Wondered what demons populated her past. 'You're right. Because what's behind us is what shapes our present. We make decisions based on what has happened to us. Learn from it. But you shouldn't dwell on it. You need to focus on the future, on your goals and dreams.' Yet that hadn't worked for him. Because now the dream, the goal he had worked towards, was out of his reach for ever. And that sucked.

'What happens if you fail?' Now her voice held a bitter undertone and her fingers curled around his palm; the touch shivered through him.

'Then you try again or you reset the goal.'

'That's not always possible.'

'No. It isn't.' His plan could never now be fulfilled and, it seemed, neither could hers.

They sat silent and he sensed a shared frustration, an instant of empathy he knew he had to dispel. He had no wish to get embroiled in anything emotional, yet the urge to do just that was nigh on overwhelming, told him to ask, to delve, to offer comfort. *Stop*. That was not his way and he could not let Emily under his skin. Instead perhaps it would be better to try to distract her, bring back the smile to stave off whatever it was in her past that had brought such sadness to her face.

'How about we set ourselves an easy-to-achieve goal? Let's walk the streets of Turin in moonlight.'

His reward a small smile and a decisive nod, the downside the bereft feeling as she gently pulled her hand away. 'That sounds wonderful.'

CHAPTER SIX

As THEY EMERGED into the dusky streets of Turin, Emily glanced up at Luca's broad outline next to her, and curiosity surfaced as she wondered at the complexity of the man. He'd been the perfect host, charming and fun, but at the end she had sensed the depth of emotions that lay behind the charming façade, wondered what had brought shadows to darken his silver-grey eyes.

As if he sensed her gaze he turned and her breath caught—he looked ridiculously handsome. Moonlight glinted his dark hair, his chiselled features etched with strength, and for a crazy moment she wanted to hurl herself against the breadth of his chest, hold him, talk to him, kiss him.

But she wouldn't. This wasn't a viable attraction. Luca's emotions were his to guard and she sensed he guarded them as fiercely as she did her own. That he too held a hurt, a dream unfulfilled, a failure he had to live with as she lived with hers. Her failure had led to tragedy, the loss of the baby she had wanted so much. Pain hurt her heart as the image of her lost baby hovered.

But she knew tonight he didn't want to dwell on it or look back, and for now neither did she. Instead she'd absorb this city with its life and laughter and traditions, focus on getting the ideas she needed.

As if his thoughts walked with hers, he gestured around. 'It's beautiful by day but it's a different sort of beautiful by night.'

Emily nodded agreement. 'A city is different by night, by day, by season…by weather. Sometimes it's happy, sometimes it's sad—I think places are fascinating and capturing different images of them is a hobby of mine. You can show such different facets—the tourist haunts and sometimes the grittier undersides.'

'I see what you mean but it would never occur to me to take a picture.'

'Of anything?' She turned to look at him, aware that incredulity had pitched her voice high. 'When is the last time you took a photo?'

'Um…' Luca frowned. 'I scanned a business document on…'

'Doesn't count.' Emily came to a halt in the middle of the street. 'Seriously, I genuinely want to know. I mean, you must take photos—nowadays you don't even need a camera. Surely you take pictures of…something. When you look around you and see such beauty don't you want to record it?'

But Luca didn't look round. Instead he looked at her; his gaze held a molten spark that tugged desire in her tummy. 'Perhaps you are right,' he said, his voice deep and decadent, and she felt a delicious sizzle of knowledge that he was saying she was beautiful. 'But sometimes I prefer to simply look at beauty. Absorb it.'

She gulped, realised she was hanging on his every word now, tugged into the depths of his eyes, intoxicated by the words, by the play of moonlight on his strong features. The catch of his accented voice added to the spell and she knew danger loomed. But somehow she couldn't bring herself to care. 'But a picture captures that beauty.'

'Or I can put it into my memory banks.'

'Memory distorts things, a picture doesn't.' Her voice sounded breathless and she realised she had stepped closer to him.

'Not true. A picture can tell a lie. Think of all the fake smiles, pictures taken to pretend everything is all right.'

'A good photographer bypasses that. If you look closely you can see the fake, it's something in the eyes, or the tilt of the lips.' Now her eyes fell to his lips, the firm contour of them, and she caught her breath.

'Fair enough, but if you are always recording a moment you aren't living it. If you look at life through a lens, then you always have something between you and reality. You're experiencing it at one remove.' The dip and cadence of his voice sent a shiver over her skin and she moved forward another step. 'It is important to experience the moment.'

'Like this?' She couldn't have stopped herself if she tried; she took one more step, placed her hands on his shoulders and kissed him. Had meant it to be a quick brushing of the lips but she hadn't reckoned on the impact, gave a small gasp of sheer delight.

And then he cupped her face gently and lowered his lips to hers again, let out a small groan and now she tasted a hint of grapefruit and the sweetness of chocolate. Then her arms went round his neck and he deepened the kiss and she was lost. The scent and sounds of the Turin night seemed to dim and mute and condense until all she was aware of was Luca and that she wanted this to last for ever.

But it couldn't. Eventually reality intruded into the bubble of sensuality. They broke apart and Emily stared at him. What had she done?

Why, oh, why had she kissed him? And how
could it be so sinfully wonderful? How could
she have been so swept away that she'd forgotten everything: professionalism and, even
worse, her grief? How could she have allowed
such joy to fizz through her—not only allowed,
but actively sought it out? The betrayal of her
grief appalled her even as her whole body still
buzzed.

'I… I have to go.' Turning, she stumbled
through the crowd. A cascade of horror at her
actions ran through her as her brain relived
the kiss, caused her to barely see the crowds
around her, the glare of the lights, the excla-
mations of annoyance. All she wanted, all she
needed, was the sanctuary of her hotel, where
she could retreat to bed and try to block this
from her mind.

'Emily. Wait.'

The sound of her name permeated the fog
of regret and she recognised Luca's voice. She
halted and spun round so quickly she almost
collided into him. Braced herself, hands up to
avoid so much as an accidental touch.

He moved to the side out of the way of pass-
ers-by. 'Emily. I am sorry.'

'You have nothing to apologise for. I kissed
you.' Anger at her own actions mingled with

the swirl of guilt that she could have been so shallow.

'And I kissed you back. That is not acceptable behaviour.' He took a deep breath. 'I want to make this right.' Emily could see the trouble in his eyes as he ran his hands through his dishevelled hair.

'*I* want to make it not to have happened. To erase it from our memory banks.' Something she suspected wouldn't be possible however much she wished it. How could she have let attraction trump common sense and simple common decency? She was grieving and her baby deserved a time of mourning. Work had become a necessity but the pursuit of pleasure had been wrong.

Luca exhaled. 'We can't pretend it never happened but…'

'We can make sure it doesn't happen again. It won't. I can assure you of that.'

He hesitated, raised a hand and dropped it again and it occurred to Emily that Luca was rattled. Clearly the kiss had affected him too and it would appear he regretted it as much as she did.

He settled for a nod. 'In that case I will meet you tomorrow morning for the tour of the factory.'

Turning, she walked almost blindly, her mind

churning with regret, her body aching with guilt. Tears threatened and she increased her pace, desperate to return to the hotel where she could lie down on the cool sheets and simply weep.

CHAPTER SEVEN

LUCA WAITED IN the hotel lobby, watched the lift doors open and Emily step out, disconcerted anew by how her beauty affected him. But today as she approached him that impact was instantly diluted by worry. There were smudges under her eyes, eyes that had a washed-out look. Had she cried herself to sleep?

And if so why? The kiss had been a mistake. He'd be the first to acknowledge that; guilt still prodded him at his own stupidity. But it didn't warrant tears. He studied her face covertly, wondered if perhaps he'd been wrong. Wished he didn't care so much, didn't feel so angry with himself that he had clearly hurt her. *Stop.* Hell, she could have got shampoo in her eyes or just slept badly.

'Good morning.' He focused on keeping his voice steady.

'Good morning.' Her voice gave nothing away, but her expression held wariness as she crossed the lobby, and as they walked through the revolving glass door he saw the effort she made to hold herself aloof so as not to risk even the smallest chance of accidental contact.

Actions he mirrored as they both climbed into the back of the car that would take them to the factory, the idea of stopping at a café for a *bicerin* now impossible. Once inside she scrunched herself as close to her side window as was humanly possible as the car pulled away from the kerb and the weight of silence descended.

Luca cleared his throat. 'The weather is a bit cloudier today.'

'Yes. Especially for this time of year.'

That seemed to cover the weather. 'I hope you will enjoy today,' he said.

'I am sure I will find it useful.' Her voice was tight, each word propped up by stilts. A pause. 'I'm looking forward to seeing where your chocolate is produced.'

Luca recalled the previous evening, the ease of their discourse, and tried to equate the woman who had shaken cocktails to the beat of Caribbean drums with the woman sitting so far away from him, her whole body taut. Regret ran through him as he cursed his own lack of restraint—he might not understand why, but the kiss had impacted her profoundly. *Come on, Luca.* It had impacted him hugely too. That kiss had broken all his own rules; in one fell swoop it had crashed through the fundamental basis of his relationship cornerstone. Do not act on attraction, do not get involved on any level until the rules were on the table. It was time to acknowledge what had happened, properly.

'No,' he said. 'You aren't looking forward to it and I wish you were. I am sorry I spoilt our professional relationship.'

'You didn't. I will still do my job to the highest standard.'

'I am sure you will, but I think what happened has made that harder.' Which was exactly why mixing professional with personal was so stupid. 'I would like to try and clear away this… awkwardness, try to make it right.'

She shook her head. 'It's hard not to feel awkward. To say nothing of embarrassed.'

'There is no need to be embarrassed. What happened between us was—'

'Unfortunate, unprofessional, unnecessary, stupid, and mortifying.'

At least this was a proper conversation. 'It was also natural.'

Suspicion frowned her face. 'What do you mean?'

'At Ava's party we clicked, did we not?'

For a moment he thought she'd deny it, then she gave a small reluctant nod. 'I suppose so.'

'I know we decided not to act on it and I know we shouldn't have but I will not be embarrassed by something natural. There is nothing wrong with feeling attraction. I agree we need to put it behind us but there is no need to be ashamed.' He studied her profile, saw that for some reason his words had had no effect. 'Look at me.' She did as he asked and he reached out and touched her lightly on the arm, pulled back fast. 'Truly, do not feel embarrassed. I do not.' That was true; he felt chagrin, surprise and annoyance and true regret at his lack of control, determination to avoid a repeat performance, but there also lingered a different regret that there wouldn't be one. Now he frowned—there were way too many feelings in the mix. So, 'How about we agree to try and be natural around each other?'

'I thought you said that was the problem in the first place.' Her tone was wry and he belatedly remembered his words of a moment ago.

'Touché,' he said and he couldn't help it, his lips turned up in a smile and suddenly she gave him an answering smile.

'But I know what you mean so, yes, let's try and put it behind us.'

'Agreed.'

The remainder of the journey was achieved in a silence, but this time it felt more comfortable.

Once at the factory they climbed out of the car and she gazed at the loom of the factory building, pulled out her camera and started to snap.

Once inside he led the way to an office. 'The contract should be in here,' he said, then picked it up from the desk and handed it over to her. Emily read it carefully and once again he found himself studying her, the smallest of creases in her forehead, the bent head supported by the graceful column of her neck.

She signed quickly and he followed suit.

'Right, let's start the tour.'

As he showed her around the factory he watched her expression, felt a sense of satisfaction at her genuine interest as he led her round the different machines and explained how each one worked. With each step, the atmosphere relaxed a little more and he could see her immerse herself in taking pictures, admired her focus and method as she made sure she got every angle.

After a while she came to a halt and, although he could still sense a slight rigidity in her posture, her expression held only interest as she returned to stand by the conching machine.

'The sheer quantity of chocolate you produce is mind-boggling... I mean, I could practically swim in it. And to think it all starts with a cocoa bean.' She glanced down at her notes. 'And so much happens to those poor beans. But, if I have it right, how they are fermented is crucial, and so is the roasting process and the conching. I'm not sure I understand that last bit.'

'Basically the mixture is stirred to extract any water that remains and to distribute the cacao butter evenly. This is what gives chocolate its taste, its texture, even its smell. The name comes from the word concha, which means shell. In the old days chocolate was conched in a vessel that was shell-shaped.'

'I really like that. I'll try to incorporate conch-shaped shells in the ads, and maybe something natural that represents the roasting and fermentation as well.'

'I'd like that.' Admiration touched him at her creative process, for the idea that the ad would embrace the actual process, would hold hints and clues that tied it all together. 'Now I see why this is so important to how you work. And now for the last bit of the tour—the tasting.'

He led the way out of the factory to the café he'd installed for meetings and tastings. Flowers hung from the rafters over the tables and the air was scented with a mixture of floral and chocolate. Once Emily was seated at one of the small wrought-iron painted tables he put together a selection of Palazzo di Cioccolato products.

'This is one of our best sellers, this is a

midnight-dark bar, here is my version of a nuts-and-raisin bar and finally here is a prototype for the new brand.'

She popped the first sample in her mouth and closed her eyes as she savoured the flavour. Luca couldn't help himself, he allowed his gaze to rove over her beautiful face, the length of her dark lashes, the slant of her cheekbones, the hue and glow of her skin. And, of course, the lips that had joined his in that explosive kiss just hours before.

Her eyes snapped open and he instantly dropped his gaze. 'What do you think?'

'These are freaking amazing. Why can't I buy your products in the UK?' She picked up the next one and took a bite. 'You are missing an enormous opportunity.'

The question was a reminder of his plan, thwarted for ever now by the finality of death. Now he would never visit Dolci headquarters, march into his father's office and issue a personal invitation to the opening of the Palazzo di Cioccolato flagship London store. Satisfy his need for revenge.

A dish best served cold and now a dish he would never get to serve at all. His dad had died and now he'd never get the chance to tell him anything. And without the idea of vengeance to fuel him the whole idea of a London store seemed pointless, filled him with a sense of flatness. Not the excitement and drive he needed to launch.

'I am planning to open in the UK. I am looking for premises in London and then I will expand to regional high streets. It's a balance between being a bit more exclusive and boutique and reaching a wider market.' He also had to summon up the enthusiasm from somewhere.

'Sure. You have already achieved so much.' She gestured towards the door that led to the factory. 'This is a massive operation. You made this happen. How? What's your story? I did look on the website but there's nothing there. What inspired you?'

Revenge. That was not an answer he would share. That he had been inspired, driven, by the need to outdo his father.

'I've always understood the importance of chocolate.' Keep it light. Give a little, but not too much. 'My mum was pregnant with Jodi and she craved chocolate. But only very good quality, expensive chocolate. I used to watch her savour the tiny squares and even then I could see that good quality chocolate was the answer.' And so the first seed of becoming a chocolatier had been planted in the close aftermath of his father's desertion, when all he'd wanted was to provide his mother with what she craved. At a time when affording basic food was a problem, and Luca could remember the gnawing pain of hunger in his belly.

Sometimes they had imagined a feast and always in that illusory meal had been chocolate; the two of them would sit and imagine the taste of it, list the ingredients, savour the imaginary taste on their tongues. The memory unsettled him and he shifted on his chair, aware of Emily's eyes on him, saw a question in hers.

'I went on a tour of a chocolate factory with school and I decided then and there that this was what I wanted to do.'

He'd looked round and wondered if the Dolci factory looked like this, full of the smell of sweetness and the churn and grind of machinery. Known he didn't want to copy his father or follow in his footsteps, he wanted to rival him.

'I managed to get a meeting with Lucio Silvetti, one of Turin's foremost chocolatiers, and he agreed to train me. I worked hard, at the cocktail bar and various other jobs, and in the end I started small and then grew the business.'

'You make it sound easy, but I know it can't have been.' Her frown deepened and she tucked a strand of hair behind her ear. 'In fact, you're making it sound boring. I don't get it. When you talk about your products and your company ethos you are full of enthusiasm. And pride.

Surely you're proud of how you achieved such success. Your story?'

'Of course, I am. But there isn't much to say about it.'

'There's loads to say about it.' A quick sideways glance at him as she picked up a crumb with her fingertip. 'Plus you don't have a photo of you on your website. I could take one now, if you like. Maybe you on the factory floor, a hands-on CEO surveying your domain.'

'No need. But thank you.' After their conversation last night he felt stupidly vulnerable, as if all his mixed feelings about his company would show in his face, in his stance, in his eyes. And maybe he could fake a smile, but Emily would know it was fake and he wasn't willing to show that to her discerning eye. For her to pick up the nuance and emotion he'd rather remain hidden. Hell, that he'd rather not feel at all. 'I prefer for my products to speak for themselves. I am more of an invisible presence.' For a moment he thought she'd protest but then she gave a small rueful smile.

'Fair enough. I guess I get that.' She placed the last piece of chocolate in her mouth and her eyes widened.

'This is absolutely amazing. I've never tasted anything quite like this.'

'That's the idea,' he said. 'I wanted to make

this different—I know some people may hate it but I'm hoping lots of people will love it.'

'I am definitely in the latter camp. It somehow combines decadent richness with refreshing lightness. How have you done that?'

He smiled and gave a mock bow. 'I told you. I'm a Zen master, remember?'

Now she laughed. 'How could I forget? But do you also think it tastes different because of the actual cocoa bean? Because it's from Jalpura and the others aren't?'

The question with its mention of Jalpura jolted him, a stark reminder of Jodi and that for the past twenty-four hours he'd barely given his sister a thought. Guilt straightened his lips into a grim line. What the hell was wrong with him? Yes, the ad campaign mattered, but not as much as Jodi. He had to keep his eye on the goal.

'I think Jalpura is definitely part of it,' he said firmly. 'So I think it's time to go there.'

CHAPTER EIGHT

EMILY SNAPPED HER seat belt on and took a deep breath as she glanced around the aeroplane. The first-class section was relatively empty of passengers so she and Luca were effectively alone, which at least meant that if her panic returned she would be free from observation. For a moment she wondered if he had deliberately orchestrated their privacy, told herself not to be foolish.

'You OK?' As he spoke he reached down into his briefcase. 'I got you this from the airport. Just in case you needed it.'

She accepted the paper bag he handed over and peered inside and a trickle of warmth touched her as she saw the content—a red squishy stress ball. 'Thank you. That is really thoughtful.' The kind of thing that would never have occurred to Howard in a million years and for some reason the gesture prickled her eyes with tears. Pulling it out, she squeezed it as the plane took off, held on tight and focused on her breathing, told herself that the sooner she got to Jalpura, the sooner she would get back.

'I hope your evening was productive?' he asked.

'It was, thank you.' She'd elected to work in her hotel room the previous night; by tacit consent neither of them had wished to spend the evening together, had no wish to risk a repeat of the kiss. 'I've put together some ideas for the ad campaign and then I sorted out my photos of Turin.' She gave a sudden smile. 'Could I be any more boring?'

'That is not boring. What do you do with all the photographs? You must have taken hundreds of images.'

'I go through, keep the best, in case I need them in the future. If I ever get asked to do a photo shoot in Turin they'll be helpful.'

'What made you choose fashion photography? I can see that you are very good at what you do but over the past days you have taken pictures of food and buildings and people, but not once have you shown any interest in actual fashion. Or gone shopping, or even window-shopped in any of the boutiques.'

His perception surprised her; the fact that he had even noticed gave her a jolt. Howard had always been focused on himself; his only concern with Emily had been how she reflected on him. Her mother's priority was always herself or her current 'love'. 'I didn't really choose it. I kind of fell into it. I've always enjoyed photography.' Her camera had been like a security blanket, a way of making invisibility a positive. She'd grown up constantly being told to 'not get in the way', 'not be noticed' by her mother. At her annual visits to her father's she'd had no idea how to fit in, had felt redundant, embarrassed, had *wanted* to be invisible. Taking photographs gave her something to do and she'd figured out that most people liked having their picture taken. And so she'd taken family photos of her dad and his second wife and their happy brood of children, all the time aware of the irony that, as the photographer, she wasn't in the snaps. A fitting representation of her role in her father's life.

'But becoming a fashion photographer was sheer dumb luck. I was at a party and the host asked if I could take some informal photos. I took one of a model and she loved it; I thought it was the booze talking but next day she called me up, told me she'd used her clout to get me a job. It all went from there. So fashion chose me really.'

'But you could have changed course if you wished.'

'It's not that easy.' She had wanted to. Had wanted to do more serious photography, the type that documented real life. The sort of work Howard did, that genuinely made a difference, showed the world the ravages of war, the injustices of poverty. That was how she and Howard had first got together. She'd somehow found the courage to approach him at a party, asked for a critique, been in super-fangirl mode. Had been stunned when he'd agreed, hadn't even cared that he'd said it was the least he could do for the daughter of a photographic icon like Marigold Turner.

'Why not?' Luca's blunt question interrupted her trip down memory lane. 'Why is it not easy?'

'It turns out my talents are better suited to the fashion industry.' Ironic but apparently true, according to Howard, and whilst her ex had many flaws Emily had understood and accepted his original critique as spot on.

'How do you know that?'

Emily glanced away, could still remember the nervous anticipation before she'd met Howard to discuss his 'verdict'—that she simply didn't have what it took, her style was too light and frothy. 'More serious stuff requires a versatility, a technique, an eye I don't have.'

Luca frowned. 'Did someone tell you that?'

'Yes, but I agree with them.'

Howard had explained it. *'You are good at what you do, Emily, in the same way an actor who is good at comedy will not be able to play Hamlet. But you should not despair, and I am sorry to be the bearer of bad news. Let me make it up to you with dinner.'*

And so it had begun.

'Photography isn't only about the type of camera or the lighting or the lens, it's about an instinct, an eye and a God-given talent. You can practise and practise and practise, but those things give you the edge. It's probably the same in the world of chocolate—not everyone can come up with the types of recipes you can. However hard they practise.'

'I get that. There are some chocolatiers born with an ability to taste and mix and judge that you can't learn. But that doesn't mean everyone will love their chocolate, because it's a matter of taste. And each person is unique—photography is not like a game of tennis where someone has to win. I don't understand why you wouldn't be able to use your talent for any type of photography. Your photographs show emotion and convey mood.'

For a second she was carried away by the force of his words, remembered vaguely that once she'd thought the same. Had held out hope that Howard might have been wrong, a hope that had eroded during the course of her marriage, under the onslaught of Howard's continued critiques, that had worsened when she'd given up her own job to be his assistant.

Until she'd accepted the truth—Howard had been right from the start—she didn't have what it took.

She shook her head. 'There is no point raising unrealistic expectations, trying to dream your dreams into reality. It's important to be realistic. I am happy with the talent I have. And I'd like to use that talent to do a good job for you.' She injected finality into her tone; she'd made her decision and she would stick to it. All her life she'd been surrounded by people of immense talent, top of their field; it had been hard to accept that she wouldn't do the same. But she had come to terms with it—decided the fact she had any talent for photography was amazing in itself; there was no need to aspire to be of Howard's calibre. 'Speaking of which, what is the plan in Jalpura?'

His gaze flicked away from her for an instant. 'I've arranged to visit the cocoa-bean farm, so you can have a tour, and we'll need to scout some locations.'

Emily studied his face, sensed a certain flatness to his voice and wondered where his usual enthusiasm had gone. 'I've already done some research into locations. There's a place where the sunsets are spectacular, and also some incredibly lush gardens and, of course, the palace. I was wondering about introducing a hint of royalty into the campaign seeing as Jalpura has a royal family.'

'That sounds great—and as though you are completely on top of it all.'

Yet again the words lacked depth, a genuine interest, and she wondered why. This project was Luca's idea, yet he looked as if his mind was focused elsewhere. Not her business. 'Speaking of which,' she said brightly, 'I'll get on with a bit more research.'

The rest of the flight was uneventful and Luca was grateful that Emily seemed content to crack on with some work, hoped she didn't notice his distraction as they approached Jalpura. Where he hoped to find answers. As they landed, went through customs and climbed into a taxi his determination grew. He would discover what had happened to Jodi.

Once they arrived at the resort, Luca looked around. He'd chosen the place because of its proximity to Jodi's last known location, a youth hostel she'd told him she'd stayed at. Though this was a far cry from a hostel. Instead of a conventional hotel a selection of thatched cottages, all side by side, surrounded an opaque turquoise swimming pool, fringed with palm trees. The air was scented with flowers and the whole place emanated an atmosphere of tranquillity.

'This is amazing.' Emily let out a small sigh of appreciation.

'I'm glad you like it. Let's settle in and meet for dinner in about an hour.'

She glanced at him, presumably surprised at the terseness of his voice, but he couldn't help it. Somehow in the past few days he'd been sidetracked from the true purpose of this trip. Had got caught up in Emily, in her company, her conversation and, of course, the fateful kiss itself. He had seen some of her vulnerabilities even if he didn't understand them and in so doing he'd lost sight of his goal to find his sister. *Not good.* His family meant everything to him. More than that, he would not break the promise he'd made himself after Lydia and the pain and humiliation of her rejection—never again would he get involved in any depth at all, never again would he put his feelings on the line.

'Dinner sounds good,' she said.

He nodded; it would give him time to contact Samar, the cocoa-farm owner, and ask him again about Jodi. See if he had remembered anything else about how she had been, whether she had mentioned anything about friends or acquaintances or plans. He would also need to request that Samar didn't mention Jodi to Emily. At this stage there was no point—after all, he might be able to discover what he needed without involving Emily at all.

Once in his cottage he pulled his phone out. 'Samar. It's Luca…'

Preliminaries over, Luca segued into what he really wanted to talk about, 'I was wondering about Jodi's visit to Jalpura. She mentioned a friend's name and I wanted to look them up, but I've lost the message Jodi sent me and I can't get hold of her at the moment. Did she mention anyone to you?'

There was a pause as Samar clearly gave the matter some thought. 'She spoke a lot about the film festival and her job there and I believe she did mention meeting the royal princess. I got the impression it was more than a meeting, more of a friendship, but I am sure you wouldn't forget that. Plus it wouldn't be that easy to just look up royalty.' A laugh travelled down the line. 'I am sorry, Luca. I cannot remember anyone else.'

'Don't worry. It isn't that important.' Royalty? Luca's brain whirred. Jodi certainly hadn't mentioned meeting royalty.

'Perhaps you could ask Jodi for an introduction,' Samar continued. 'Get royal endorsement for your chocolate.'

'I'll do that. Thank you. And, could I ask a favour? Please do not mention Jodi in front of Emily tomorrow. There is a slightly complicated situation going on and...'

'You do not need to explain, my friend. Women are complicated.'

Goodbyes said, Luca disconnected and began to pace as he tried to figure out what to do with this new information, wished that Samar had recalled it when he'd spoken to him weeks before to question him. It was a slim lead that might lead nowhere but it was better than nothing and he would definitely follow it up.

A glance at his watch and he headed to the door, exited his cottage and headed for Emily's. He'd keep dinner quick and get back to do some research into the Jalpuran royal family.

He knocked on Emily's door, braced himself for the impact. She truly did stun him anew every time he saw her and he wished she didn't. Didn't understand the visceral punch and it unsettled him that he couldn't seem to douse or control it.

'Ready?' he asked.

'Ready.' Dressed in black smart trousers and a tunic top, she looked perfectly presentable in her usual understated way. He sensed it was deliberate, that she dressed to eschew attention, to deflect notice.

She picked up a small evening bag from the table by the door and stepped outside into the balmy scented evening, pulled the door shut behind her.

He led the way to the outdoor terrace where tables dotted the mosaic tiles and it was only now, as a waiter materialised, pulled out their chairs, lit candles and provided menus, that he really took in the setting and its implications. The scent of frangipani rode gently on the air, the flicker of candles added to the twinkle of the fairy lights that artfully bedecked the surroundings. The tables were placed discreet distances apart and as he glanced around he saw the place was full of couples. And for a crazy moment he imagined that he and Emily were here together as a couple, that he had the right to lean across the table and brush his lips against hers, to hold her hand as they chose their meals, to play footsie under the table.

Resolutely he turned his attention to the menu just as the waiter approached, held out a basket filled with garlands of flowers. 'Would you like to choose one for your beautiful lady?' he asked.

He saw Emily open her mouth to deny the need but all of a sudden Luca wanted to choose some flowers, wanted her to put them in her hair or round her neck. To jazz up the plainness of her outfit and show off her beauty. 'Of course,' he said and studied the different choices, settled on a white jasmine, took it out and leaned across the small intimate table and carefully tucked it into her hair, felt his fingers tremble at the feel of her silken strands, heard her breath catch too.

Leaning back, he surveyed his handiwork. 'Beautiful,' he said. The waiter beamed at them both and moved away.

'You didn't need to say that. I mean, you're right, it's probably easier to let them think we're a couple like everyone else here. But there's no need to overdo it.'

'I wasn't. I was simply stating a fact. You do look beautiful.'

He'd swear she shifted slightly on her seat, looked more than a touch uncomfortable. 'Thank you. I guess.'

'It's not an insult.'

'I know.'

'Then why has it made you so uncomfortable?'

'I told you, I don't think looks are relevant.'

'So, if we were a couple you wouldn't want me to say you look beautiful?'

'I…' Her eyes narrowed. 'It's a moot point. Because we aren't a couple.' That was true enough, so what was he doing? Yet she was beautiful and for some reason he wanted her to know that. But Emily continued to speak. 'Unlike everyone else here. It's like Romance Central, Cupid's arrows darting everywhere.' Her voice held more than a hint of disparagement and he decided to go with the opportune change in subject.

'Perhaps those arrows are missing their mark. Or these people could be here desperately trying to spice up a dead marriage, or this is what they do every year and they are utterly bored, or they could be plotting a divorce or a murder...'

'OK, Mr Cynic. I'm guessing romance isn't your thing.'

'No.' His gaze rested on the flower he'd just put in her hair. 'It's not.' The words almost over-emphasised, a reminder to himself.

She raised her glass of water. 'Good call.' She tipped her head to one side. 'So this isn't the sort of place you'd bring a partner on holiday.'

'I wouldn't bring a partner anywhere on holiday. That's not the way my arrangements work.'

'Arrangements?' Her nose wrinkled as she looked at him questioningly, tucked an errant strand of hair behind her ear, the movement fluid and familiar, and for some reason it tugged at something in his chest. His gaze lingered on the flower in her hair, the contrast of colour, the delicate shape of the petals against the silky softness. And a memory of their shared kiss suddenly blasted his brain. Perhaps this would be a good time to remind himself of his relationship rules, demonstrate exactly how far out of bounds Emily was.

'Basically I date women who fit a certain criteria, who are looking for the same things that I am. A relationship where we enjoy each other's company every so often but without clinginess or neediness on either side. No expectations other than an entertaining dinner companion, a bed partner, someone to take to social functions. The occasional night away but definitely not a holiday.'

'But how do you keep it like that—surely if its long-term you get to know each other better over time, start to like each other more?'

He shook his head. 'I'm talking about meeting up once, maybe twice a month. Not keeping toothbrushes at each other's place. The essence is that it's low-key, not intense. Fun and easy. Nothing heavy.' It was a system he had perfected after his break-up with Lydia. A system devised to ensure no investment in deep emotion, dependency or love. That way there was zero risk of hurting or being hurt. One thing was certain: Luca Petrovelli would never open himself up to the risk of abandonment again.

He could spot a pattern when he saw one: first a father he had loved and then a girlfriend he'd adored. 'That way no one gets hurt.'

'But you can't guarantee that.'

'I can try. I take care to only date women who are not emotionally vulnerable. For example, I would not date someone who has recently been in a relationship.'

She waited until the waiter came and took their orders and then leaned forward. 'But what if a woman wants something different from you?'

'Then she shouldn't date me. I am upfront from the beginning as to what I can offer and what I want in return. And I do my best to make sure any woman who I date truly wants the same.'

'But how can you be sure of that? You seem to want a fun, low-maintenance woman with no emotional needs at all. Does that exist?'

'Yes. There are women who are not interested in a happy ever after. I don't want to get caught up in anyone's desire for love—I won't hold them back on their quest. Neither will I pretend or con them into believing I am something I'm not. That I'll be there for them on a weekly or daily basis. Equally I don't expect them to be there for me. It works and there are plenty of plus points. Enjoyable dates with no pressure, relaxed conversations, sharing a nice time.'

Worry etched Emily's features. 'Are you in one of those relationships now?'

'No. If I was then I would not have kissed you.' In truth he should not have kissed her anyway; she didn't fit his criteria, was not a woman he had discussed his relationship rules with and yet it hadn't stopped him. Even now as he looked at her across the table the desire to kiss her again simmered inside him and he clenched his jaw in frustration. With Emily he was breaking rules; worst of all they were his own rules. 'My arrangements may lack emotion, but they involve fidelity.' That was important. 'I would never betray that trust.'

'So what happened with your last arrangement?'

He sipped his beer. 'Georgia worked for an international company—she got an assignment overseas.'

'And you didn't mind?'

'Not at all. I was happy for her—it was a promotion she'd worked hard for and she deserved it. We said goodbye and wished each other well.'

'How long had you been "together"?'

'About eighteen months. But we'd probably only seen each other twenty times in total over that time. She travelled a lot for work.'

'And before that?'

'Marina broke it off—she met someone else.'

'And that didn't bother you?'

'No, that's the beauty of this. No one gets hurt.'

'But it's also sad. The idea of these women moving on and not having made enough of an impact on your life for you to even care.'

The comment jolted him; he'd never thought about it like that and for a moment he felt strangely diminished inside, as if he lacked something important. A notion he dismissed promptly. 'But that's way better than them moving on and I am left devastated.' This he knew.

'Has that happened to you? Have you been left devastated?' she asked.

'Just the once. It falls under the young and foolish category, so perhaps devastation is a bit of an exaggeration. I was twenty, I fell in love and Lydia moved on to someone richer and more successful.' An echo of his father's actions.

'That sucks.'

'It did, but I really only had myself to blame.' He should never have lost control of his feelings, should never have let the feelings flourish and grow into love.

'Had you been together long?'

'Six months. I was working at Silvio's and she used to come in for a cocktail. We got talking and it spiralled from there.' He'd fallen and fallen hard, tried to resist but in the end he had

succumbed, decided that he and Lydia were
the exception to the rule, that happy ever afters
were possible. 'Unfortunately she didn't feel the
same way I did. I walked into work one day and
she was kissing one of the customers. Harry Ch-
isholm. His dad was a millionaire and he lived
a way more exciting lifestyle than I did.'

He could still feel the raw pain he'd felt then,
as he'd stood rooted to the spot, watching the
kiss. It had been Lydia who had spotted him,
who had broken away. She had taken Harry by
the hand and they'd approached him.

*'I'm sorry you had to find out like this. I've
been trying to work out how to tell you.'*

Harry had left them alone and Lydia had
continued to speak. Luca had been unable to
say anything, the rawness of his pain new, yet
all too familiar. There had been sadness in her
voice.

*'I'm truly sorry, Luca. But you're so serious,
so focused on your business and your training
and work. Harry is fun and exciting and—'*

'Rich.'

He'd managed the syllable, infused it with all
the bitterness he'd felt.

*'And he's charming...and he doesn't take life
so...personally.'*

The words had cut him to the heart, a reminder
of his childhood self. This was his fault—just as

it had been his fault his dad had left. There was something wrong with him.

'I'm sorry, Luca.' Emily's voice, gentle and full of compassion, pulled him to the present.

'Don't be. It's an old story—it happens all the time to millions of people. It was no big deal, but I will admit it put me off love and romance.'

'I understand why. But I think there is a different solution to your arrangements.'

'Such as?'

Before she could reply the waiter approached their table.

CHAPTER NINE

As the waiter put the aromatic plates in front of them Emily reflected on what Luca had shared; it might be an old story, but she sensed that eighteen-year-old boy would have been devastated by Lydia's behaviour. Sensed too that he would rather walk on hot coals than admit it, and wanted to give him a bit of a time out to walk away from the memory of Lydia.

Emily looked down at her plate, inhaled the delicious scent of spices, garlic, fresh green chilli and cumin and couldn't help but admire the presentation of her *sadhya*—a variety of curries and dals and pickles in small stainless-steel pots all arranged on a banana leaf. She looked across at Luca's choice, a rice-flour pancake filled with a curry that emitted the waft of ginger and coconut.

'Do you mind if I take a picture of yours as well as mine?'

'No problem.'

A few minutes later, she gave a small sigh of satisfaction and took her first taste. 'This is beyond amazing.'

He nodded. 'Mine too. Do you want to try some?'

'Yes, please.' She waited whilst he sectioned off a bit of his and moved it onto her plate, 'And help yourself.' She tore of a piece of chapati and handed it over, watched as he dipped it into one of the pots and she revelled in the strange intimacy of sharing food.

For a few moments they savoured the dishes, and then he wiped his mouth on a napkin. 'So what is your solution to relationships? You tried marriage so I assume you believe in the happy-ever-after theory. Or at least you did.'

'Definitely past tense.' There had been no happiness in the ending with Howard. Even now the sequence of events was a horrible blur. Her pregnancy had been a surprise but to Emily it had been a welcome one. To Howard it had not; and as her pregnancy had progressed his displeasure had only increased. His insistence she conceal it, his growing impatience, his disparaging remarks. All had culminated in her discovery that he was sleeping with someone else. The scale of her anger at his betrayal still shocked her, their confrontation a humdinger that she regretted with all her heart, because two weeks later she'd lost the baby and a part of her believed that somehow the sheer raw pain and exhaustion could have caused it.

Her pain must have shown on her face because Luca leaned forward and, oh, so gently took her hands in his. 'I'm sorry. I didn't mean to bring back memories or hurt you.'

'It's OK. Truly. It was a painful break-up but I have put Howard behind me now.' Not her baby, she would never ever be able to do that, would never want to. 'And I won't repeat past mistakes, I'm done with love.' She wouldn't make the same mistakes as her mother. 'But your type of arrangements wouldn't work for me. If I am with someone I want to feel I am important enough that they would at least miss me if I were gone. Or at the very least notice— it doesn't sound as though Georgia or Marina impacted on your life at all.'

He shook his head. 'They didn't in the sense that they had the power to hurt me. But I did like them, and they liked me—we did have good times together.'

'But they didn't matter.'

'No,' he agreed. 'That was the point. Once a person matters to you then you open yourself to pain and hurt.'

'Agreed.' She'd seen her mother hurt time and again and after each disaster she'd got back up on her feet and entered the fray again, her quest for love undimmed. 'It's no secret that my mother has been married multiple times and it seems to me that she never learns; she opens herself up time and again to the same type of man in her search for love.'

When Emily had remonstrated, Marigold had simply pointed out that she wasn't a quitter.

'I'll never give up on true love and my happy ending.'

'But my father—he did learn from his marriage to my mother. His second marriage works perfectly. He and Neela do matter to each other but not too much.' Rajiv Khatri had married Neela very soon after he split with Marigold and his second wife couldn't be more different from his first.

'How so?'

'Their relationship works because it isn't based on grand passion, or whirlwind romance. It's practical and nice and comfortable—they care about each other but without the angst.' There were no fights, no raised voices and a sense of calm politeness. 'They like and respect each other and they are both happy doing their own separate things. Neela goes with him to some of the Bollywood parties but she doesn't mind if he goes on his own. Neela is involved with charity work and Dad helps out with that if he can. But she spends a lot of time on that. And, of course, they have a family.' The words were a reminder of what she had hoped for just months before, and what she'd lost—the chance of a family of her own. *Not now.* 'That is definitely Neela's priority. And Dad's. They put their family first.'

As a child she had watched the loving, nurturing bond Neela had with her children, realised that she prioritised them, thought about them, planned for them. And it had been nearly impossible not to compare it with her own relationship with her mother. It would never occur to Marigold to put Emily first. At the start of each new relationship, throughout each marriage, Marigold put her man first, relegated Emily to second tier. There was the time she had been bundled off to boarding school, only to be taken back out to comfort Marigold when the marriage collapsed. The time a live-in nanny had been employed, until said nanny had an affair with husband number three.

'What you are describing…in a way your father and Neela have found love.'

'They have found affection. That would be enough for me.' Along with a family. The beauty would be that she would be able to prioritise her children, put them before romantic love. Put them first in a way she never had been by either of her parents. In some ways, she hadn't put her baby first—instead she had been swayed by her misplaced love for Howard.

'So really you want an arrangement too. But with a bit more depth.'

Emily considered the words, then acknowledged the truth. 'A lot more depth. I want to be with someone I like and respect and who will be a good father to our children. Will put them first. It would be a good arrangement. Maybe you should consider it.' Belated realisation of how he might take her words hit her. 'Not with me, obviously.'

Amusement glinted in his eyes. 'So that's not a proposition?' The words were said with a smile that curled her toes and the mood morphed and suddenly the air seemed heavy with possibility.

'Of course not!' Yet scenarios triggered in her imagination—herself and Luca surrounded by a brood of children. A dark-haired boy with brown eyes, a dark-haired girl, hair in plaits, with Luca's grey eyes. Emily sat holding a tiny baby in her arms, Luca looking down on them with a smile in his eyes.

Holy Moly. Where had all that come from? Yet as she looked at Luca, desperately tried to keep any vestige of her thoughts from her face, she saw something in his eyes and for a treacherous moment she wondered, hoped, that it was a mirror of her own stupid vision.

Enough. For the first time in twenty-four hours panic started to ripple in the deep dark pool of guilt. How could she sit here picturing a new family, a new baby, in such vivid detail? It was only a year since tragedy had struck. Since the miscarriage that had sent her spinning downward.

'Emily.' Now Luca's voice was laced with concern. 'I apologise—it was simply a joke and a bad one at that. I know you are not propositioning me.'

'I know you know.' Seeing the dawn of questions she didn't want to answer, the flash of concern in his silver-grey eyes, she pulled her unravelled thoughts together, pushed back at the panic until it subsided, sank a little towards the depths. 'I just thought maybe you should consider a different type of arrangement, one that allows you to have a family.'

'Nope. It's still too high risk. For me, as a man. If my wife were to leave the odds are that she would take the children, would have custody. And maybe I would not deeply love my wife, but I would love my children. That love would give any woman too much power over me. The power to take them away from me.'

Emily heard the depth of passion in his voice,

knew he meant it. That this man would rather not have children at all than risk losing them. And how could she blame him? His father had abandoned his family; why wouldn't his wife abandon him? And he was right. Her arrangement would work better for a woman; she would most likely have custody of any children.

So, 'I get that.' Her voice was quiet and he looked at her with raised brows.

'You do?'

'Yes. You don't ever want to settle for being a part-time father.' As her own father had been. In truth Emily knew she was a redundant child—he had five others and his interest in Emily was a duty only. 'And you won't risk the pain of having your kids taken away from you.' She looked down at her empty plate. 'I understand, but I think you're wrong.'

'Why?'

How to explain it? Explain that despite the pain, the misery, the gut-wrenching, soul-searing sense of loss she wouldn't undo her baby, wouldn't take away her pregnancy? She couldn't explain that without telling Luca of her grief and she wasn't ready to do that.

'Because I believe the chance to be a parent is worth any risk. And because I believe, even if you were a part-time father, you'd make it work somehow. If you wanted to.' This man would make anything work. If he wanted to.

There was a silence and then he shook his head. 'I don't want to and the best way to ensure that is not to start that sort of relationship. I think I'll steer clear of love of any kind.'

'I am not advocating love. Love is a chimera and an illusion, the holy grail that people chase, a word they bandy about when really it's all about attraction, or money, or fame... I've always known that. But when I met Howard I forgot the rules, forgot what I know deep in my bones. I got conned by the illusion. Never again.' She gave a sudden laugh. 'Listen to me. In the most romantic place in the world, denouncing love.'

He raised his glass. 'To non-romance.'

'I'll drink to that.'

Once they'd clinked she said, 'Now how about we talk about something completely different? What's the detailed itinerary for tomorrow? Cocoa-bean farm in the afternoon? And I was thinking about visiting the royal palace gardens in the morning.'

Luca's reaction was palpable; his forehead creased into a frown and his lips thinned.

'Unless that doesn't work for you? There's no need for you to come to the gardens.'

'It's not that. You simply reminded me of

something.' Something important, clearly. 'Samar, the owner of the farm suggested I get royal endorsement for the chocolate.'

'That's a great idea.' But it did not explain the reason for the grim set to his lips or the fierceness of his scowl.

'I just need to work out the best person to approach.' His frown intensified as he glanced at his watch. 'If it's OK with you I think I'll call it a night. I'd better get on with some research and putting a proposal together for this endorsement.'

'Sure.' She tried not to feel hurt at the abruptness. 'I've got work to do too.'

Ten minutes later she said goodbye to Luca and entered the cottage, looked round the clean, cool, uncluttered interior. Wicker furniture and white cushions, a sleek wooden desk and a sumptuous double bed.

But she wasn't tired—a mix of jet lag and a reaction to the conversation she'd just had. Perhaps work would help; she could research tourist spots or finish putting together her Turin photos. As she booted up her computer and pulled up the images she paused, she hovered over a rare shot she had got of Luca. He'd been in the shot accidentally and in fact that made it way better than a posed one. He had been explaining something in the factory, the art of roasting a cocoa bean, and you could see passion and integrity and pride in his stance and features. It would be perfect for his website. Whatever he thought.

Emily frowned and quickly pulled up the website of Palazzo di Cioccolato to study it again, as an idea gathered in her mind.

Luca awoke the following morning, aware of a strange sense of anticipation. As he swung his legs out of bed he assured himself his mood had nothing to do with Emily Khatri and everything to do with having done something constructive about Jodi.

The previous night he had researched the royal family and the recent film festival. Nowhere had he found any mention of his sister, but he now understood two royal family trees. The Jalpuran one and that of the Mediterranean island of Talonos. The Royal Film Festival was held on each island biannually and covered both Bollywood and European films. The royals from Talonos fronted the European side.

So in terms of friendships, assuming Jodi had been befriended by the younger royals, this narrowed it down on the Jalpuran side to Prince Rohan, Princess Alisha and Princess Riya and on the Talonosian side to Prince Carlos and Prince Juan.

Obviously contacting royalty wasn't straightforward but he had emailed the royal representative to ask for a meeting about an endorsement. At the meeting, what could be more natural than to mention Jodi? And the beauty of it was there would be no need to involve Emily at all, no need to use her name.

So now he could go and enjoy his time with Emily with a clear conscience. The words replayed in his head. Enjoy his time? No. What he meant was he could focus on the ad campaign. This was business, not a date. He and Emily wanted diametrically different things from a relationship and he would not forget that. Would never risk hurting someone else, especially Emily, who had clearly been hurt badly before. The memory of the sadness in her stance and face brought a frown to his face. If it had been Howard who had caused such hurt, he would take great pleasure in kicking the man round Jalpura, globally renowned photographer or not.

Once dressed in chinos and a T-shirt he left the cottage and headed to the outdoor restaurant area, which had been transformed from its night-time ambience. Now the sun shone on the grass-thatched canopy that trailed flowers down the stilted sides that propped it up. The air was replete with the smell of coffee and an aroma of spice emanated from the heaving buffet table set up to one side.

He waved as he saw Emily emerge from her cottage and soon they were seated. He glanced at her, sensed a certain lightness in her mood and he smiled. Her return smile was so sweet he blinked, felt warmth touch his chest. 'This looks sumptuous,' she said. 'I can't believe I can even eat after last night, but I can.'

They headed for the buffet and returned with heaped plates. 'It's strange to eat spicy food at breakfast but somehow here it works.' Emily spooned tomato chutney onto a piece of her *dosa*.

'Last time I came here I vowed I'd learn how to cook some of these recipes.'

'Have you?'

'Unfortunately not.' He'd got home and soon after that his world had imploded with the death of his father.

'Do you cook a lot?'

'A fair bit; I like coming up with new recipes, but nothing on this scale.' He looked down at his plate with the *idlis*—rice flour cakes served with a spicy *dal sambar*.

They ate in silence after that, both savouring the tastes until, once replete, Emily spread a map of the island on the table.

'Right, the Royal Palace Gardens are here.

I reckon we've got time for a couple of hours there before we head to the farm.'

'Sounds good. Let's go.'

Half an hour later they approached the lush green hill and looked towards the apex where the palace sprawled in an ungainly beauty. The red-orange walls were dappled with flecks of sunshine and the multi-faceted windows reflected myriad motes of light.

For a moment Luca wondered if Jodi's friend was inside somewhere, a person who could give him the answers he sought, and then he was distracted as Emily made a sweeping gesture that encompassed lush landscaped meadows, flowering shrubs and bamboo thickets.

'This definitely has potential.'

'Yes.' He looked down at her and for a bitter-sweet moment it seemed to him as though her words applied to them, that somehow in a different universe and time they had potential to be something more than business colleagues. But not in this one, for all the reasons they had enumerated only hours before.

'Especially if you want the hint of royalty. Either way I'll take some good focused shots of the palace and grounds.'

He watched as she clicked away, camera shutter whirring. She paused, looked up at the palace. 'I wonder what history those walls have seen. And what sort of life goes on in there now.'

So, ironically enough, did he.

'Anyway, I think I've got enough. Are there any particular angles you think I may have missed? Would you like a shot of you?'

'No. I'm good, thank you. I'm sure you have it covered and I'm sure we don't need a picture of me to sell chocolate.'

Emily took a deep breath. 'Actually, I want to talk to you about that. I…well, I've had an idea.'

'Go ahead.' He indicated a bench and they sat down.

'I think you *would* sell your chocolate.' She pulled her phone out of her pocket and quickly scrolled down to a photo of him in the factory in Turin. 'This would look great on your website. It could be part of your story. It shows how much you care, your passion for what you create. I think that will make people buy your products. People like the personal touch. You could have a photo of you with your mentor, the famous chocolatier, pictures of you mixing ingredients, on the cocoa farm. I'm happy to do it.'

He watched her expression, the way the light played on her skin, her excitement at the idea, the expressive wave of her hands and he wanted to encourage that, wanted to agree, but he couldn't. He had always vowed never to do what his father had done—bind his product to his name. 'I told you, Emily, *I* don't want to be on the website. I prefer being an invisible presence.'

'But why?' Now she twisted to face him, her brown eyes studying his expression as her forehead creased in puzzlement. 'You have achieved so much, Luca. It's…incredible and, damn it, I bet loads of people want to know how you did it, want the personal touch. The Petrovelli brand. The Petrovelli story.'

'I prefer to remain out of the public eye,' he said.

She shook her head and he could see hurt dawn in her eyes. 'It's OK. Obviously you have your reasons and you don't want to share them. I thought it would be a good idea. Sorry I overstepped.'

Damn it. Luca tried to tell himself he hadn't asked Emily to waste her time on this, that this wasn't his fault. But as she stood up and hitched her camera onto her shoulder he knew he wanted to erase the hurt from her gaze. He suspected she'd been hurt enough recently, knew she'd taken the rejection personally as a slur on her ability.

'You didn't. And I truly love your ideas. But I can't do it—tell the Petrovelli story. You think I should do what my father did, and I understand that it's a great marketing strategy.' Dolci's success had been part founded on marketing the Casseveti name, the entrepreneur husband, the aristocratic beautiful wife, the cute Casseveti heiress, the celebrity lifestyle. 'But the whole Casseveti fairy tale was built on a foundation of betrayal, on my mother's misery and abandonment. The Petrovelli story is the flipside of the Casseveti coin. When my father left we had nothing.' His mother had refused to take anything, had too much pride, 'Then my mother realised she was pregnant. That chocolate I told you about that she craved—do you want to know why she was so restrained when she ate it? Because there was only one small bar, and even that I begged from the shop owner. When it was gone, we sat and listed the ingredients together, closed our eyes and imagined the taste. That's how my love of chocolate started. And I'll be damned if I put that on the website.'

She sat back down on the bench, turned towards him, her focus now solely on him. 'I'm sorry. I assumed your father supported you, or at least made some sort of settlement.' The compassion on her face was almost painful and he didn't want it. This was exactly why he didn't share his background. He did not want pity, remembered it etched on the man who owned the chocolate shop all those years ago, on the faces of anyone who ever discovered they were Cassevetis, the pauper outcasts of the Dolci brand. Remembered the bullying, all brought about because a playground thug had seen an article on the Cassevetis.

But all that was over. 'There is no need to be sorry. It doesn't matter any more. It is best forgotten.'

'No, it isn't. Because it makes your story all the more amazing. You built Palazzo di Cioccolato from nothing, built it on a foundation of guts and determination. And I bet your mum is proud of you.'

Now he was on easier ground. 'She is amazing; I couldn't have done it without her. She didn't let what my father did make her bitter. And she always put us first. Looking back, I know how terrified she must have been, how lost and lonely. I do remember her crying a lot but always when she thought I couldn't hear her. And somehow she picked herself up and supported us. Found a way to put food on the table. She worked in some terrible places, but she also studied, did evening courses and now she is a high-flying lawyer. And somehow through all of it she was always there for us, to help with homework, to talk to us, to support us.'

'She sounds wonderful.'

'She is. Jodi and I are lucky.'

'Yes, you are. Truly lucky.' For a second she looked away into the distance and her wistful voice made him wonder what her own relationship with her mother was like. 'So why not put that on your website? A tribute to your mum, a picture of you and her, part of your story to honour her strength.'

'No. I won't do that; I won't do what my father did, spin a sugary story of love and devotion and family. I do love my family—I would do anything for my mother, for Jodi. Anything. But I will not use that love and turn it into a publicity stunt to sell my product. Our family life is private.' Even now he wasn't sure he understood what his mum had gone through, but he knew he wouldn't expose her or Jodi in any way to the public eye.

'I didn't mean it like that.' Emily's voice was small and he realised he'd sounded harsher than he meant. 'I meant I truly think your mum is fantastic. Not all mums put their kids first.'

He recalled her words from yesterday, the allusion to her mum's multiple marriages, her desire to have the type of arrangement where she put her family first, and he spoke without thought, 'I guess yours didn't?' He shook his head. 'Sorry. Now *I* have overstepped.'

'It's OK. You're right. Don't get me wrong, my mum loves me, she does, but she didn't put me first. Not when it came to her relationships—she seemed to always fall for men who had no interest in children. So I became a nuisance; she was worried I'd get in the way, drive them away, and she wanted to focus her whole being on her new man.'

'That can't have been easy.' The idea of a young Emily being shunted out of the way, made to feel like an unwanted impediment, made him both angry and sad.

As if she sensed this, she gave a quick shake of her head. 'It wasn't, but it wasn't the end of the world either. In all fairness to Mum, she had never planned on being a parent, and she does her best. When she isn't pursuing love or getting over a broken heart Mum is loads of fun to be with. I have plenty of good childhood memories.' She met his gaze, her chin jutting out. 'So there is no need to be sorry,' she said, echoing his own words of a few minutes before, and he realised she wanted pity as little as he did.

'I understand that, and I am glad you and your mum do have a positive relationship.' He admired the way Emily took the good and didn't bemoan the bad.

'And I am glad that you succeeded and now you can provide your mum with as much chocolate as she wants. You started a business off your own back with strength and resolve, not helped by family friends or inherited wealth. And you should be proud of that.' She tilted her head to one side. 'But you aren't, are you? When you talk about your company, your passion and pride is unmistakeable. But you must be equally proud of yourself.'

Her words jolted through him. 'Of course, I am.' But the words lacked conviction even to him. Even if that didn't make sense. He'd been driven all his life to be a success, to rival his father, and until this moment he'd have sworn he was damn proud of his journey. Just because he didn't want to publicise his story didn't mean he wasn't proud of it. Did it? Emotions began to swirl inside him, triggered by the sincerity of Emily's gaze as she continued to speak.

'What you have achieved is…superlative. You've built your company up on talent, guts and determination.'

Luca listened to the words, saw admiration in the depths of her brown eyes and the truth hit him: the realisation that he didn't deserve admiration or accolades from this woman. From anyone.

His voice was harsh as he spoke. 'Palazzo di Cioccolato isn't built on guts and determination and talent. It's built on revenge. All I wanted was to outdo my father.' The whole raison d'être of this company was to defeat James Casseveti.' And now bitterness pervaded his voice as he realised that, whilst he'd prided himself on getting over his dad, in truth his whole life's work had been governed by James. Frustrated anger roiled through him.

'Then you made something positive out of something negative.' She leant forward, placed a hand on his arm, and he caught his breath; her touch diminished the anger as warmth entered the mix. She looked up at him and his heart twisted at the serious look in her eyes, the depth of belief. 'What your father did to your mother, to you, was wrong. You could have taken that negativity and desire for revenge and done something bad with that. Instead you did good. You found a talent inside yourself and you have made a success of your life. Of your company and yourself.'

How he wanted to believe her, but emotions twisted his gut. How could he be proud? Because in the end he'd failed. Death had robbed him of the revenge he'd dreamed of and he was left knowing his life's purpose could never now be achieved.

Her hand moved from his arm and slipped

into his and she squeezed gently. 'Be proud of your story, Luca. I would be.'

'Even if it ended in failure. In the end I never had my chance to show my dad that I made it. Without him. He'll never see me set up my flagship London store. I'll never send him an invite to the opening party.' He gave a small mirthless laugh. 'It sounds stupid, does it not? That was my life goal.'

'No. It doesn't sound stupid. But you didn't fail. The very act of living your life as you have, of being a true family with your mum and Jodi, all you have achieved despite what he did to you all—that is success and you mustn't let anything take that away from you.' She continued, 'Set up your London flagship store and dedicate it to your mother, to your own success. Full stop.'

As he saw the conviction on her face for the first time in a long time he felt a small buzz of enthusiasm about a London launch, a faint sensation, but it was there, and he took her hand in his, squeezed it gently. 'Thank you. I will think about it.'

'I'm glad.' Her smile was so warm it seemed to envelop him with a sense of well-being, a lightness that prompted him to lean forward and brush his lips against her cheek. Her closeness, her scent, the tickle of her hair all combined to whirl his head, the impact somehow equal to when he had really kissed her.

He heard her intake of breath, knew he had to break this spell, had to change the dynamic to one he actually understood. Pulling away gently, he rose to his feet, made a show of glancing at his watch. 'We'd better get going. The farm awaits.'

CHAPTER TEN

THE JOURNEY TO the farm held Emily speechless; the sheer verdant lushness of the landscape took her breath and all her energy as she frantically tried to capture it on film, relieved to have something to do, something to focus on other than Luca. Something had happened back there—somehow they'd both ended up sharing and she wasn't sure how or why.

'Don't forget to also look and take it in,' Luca recommended from beside her and after a while she did just that. Hills gently undulated against a background of majesty where mountains loomed in the distance, the rush of water from a waterfall vied with the cacophony of the wildlife and in the end she simply watched as the vivid, vibrant scenery flashed past. Forest dark and thick with deciduous green, the dip and rise of dense valleys spun her head with the sheer force of nature.

Until they reached the farm itself, where she

took in the sweet fragrant scents of coconut and the rich smell of soil and earth. She walked with Luca to the whitewashed house where she knew Samar lived and worked.

Before they could knock the door swung open and a man emerged. Grizzled salt-and-pepper hair, dark, weather-beaten skin and deep-set eyes creased with laughter lines, he stepped towards Luca, a smile on his face.

'Welcome, Luca.'

Luca moved into a quick embrace, stood back and the two men clasped hands, and instinctively Emily held her camera up, snapped the picture even as she asked permission.

'No problem.'

Luca gestured to Emily. 'This is Emily. Emily, Samar.'

'I am happy to meet you,' Samar said, his English fluent and his smile wide.

'Me too. I am so excited to see your farm; from everything Luca has told me, I understand that your beans inspired his new brand and I am stoked to see where it all started.'

'I am happy for Luca to show you around and then please come back here for tea and cakes.' Samar turned to Luca. 'All the staff have been told of your coming and your requirements.'

Emily frowned. Had there been some sort of secret message, an emphasis on the word requirement, or was it simply because Samar spoke English as a second language?

Luca smiled easily. 'Thank you. Is it OK for Emily to take photographs anywhere or are there any areas we should stay away from?'

'Feel free to go anywhere. Many of the workers do not speak English but I can answer any questions you have later.'

'Thank you.' Emily smiled, instinctively liking the middle-aged farm owner, his face weathered from the sun and the callouses on his hands indicating that he did his fair share out in the fields. She followed Luca back to the car and they drove down a dusty track that led to the farm itself and groves of trees.

'The taller ones are coconut trees,' Luca explained as he parked on the verge and they climbed out. 'They provide shelter for the cocoa trees that have been planted between them. The trees are quite delicate and keeping them thriving is a huge part of Samar's responsibility. They need to be protected from wind and sun, the soil needs to be fertilised correctly and any sign of damage or disease has to be dealt with quickly. Samar once said to me that he sees these trees like his marriage. He has been married for forty years...since he was seventeen.'

'Wow.' She contemplated the idea, and for a scant second she envied it.

'Samar believes that marriages need work and effort to thrive and bear fruit. He says nowadays people give up too easily.'

Emily thought of her mother on marriage number five, of her own disastrous marriage to Howard. 'The problem is that it takes two people to do the work. It can't all be done by one person.' Her mother had put so much effort into each relationship, made sure she always looked perfect, relegated Emily to the background, thrown herself into every husband's hobbies, tried to support them all to no avail. And, irony of irony, Emily, having vowed she never would, had followed exactly in her mother's footsteps.

'Exactly. That's why I stand by what I said yesterday. On your own you are in control, in a partnership you have to rely on someone else. Samar relies on these trees to respond to his care, he relies on the weather, on luck, on so many variables. Plus he has to put a lot in before he gets anything out. These trees don't yield pods at all for a few years.'

'What is their yield?'

'A typical pod contains thirty to forty beans and there are about thirty pods per tree. It takes about four hundred dried beans to make one pound of cocoa.'

She stopped and looked at the trees, studied their shape, the clusters of pink and white flowers that dotted the branches and trunks, the green pods that dipped from the branches. She wanted to take photographs that emphasised their beauty, productivity and fragility, how susceptible they were to nature. That they needed care and nurture to flourish.

'I wish I could get up closer. I mean, I can zoom in, but I want to actually touch the pods, get the texture and the feel. Do you reckon I can climb it?'

'No.' His voice held a hint of amusement. 'The bark is soft and quite fragile. At harvest they use long-handled steel tools to reach and cut the pods so they don't damage it.'

'Hmm. Climbing is definitely out.'

'Not necessarily. You can climb up and sit on my shoulders.'

She knew, with absolute certainty, he'd spoken without thinking, simply made a practical suggestion.

There was a silence and she eyed his shoulders, their breadth and strength, imagined sitting astride them, legs dangling over his chest, him steadying her by wrapping his hands around her calves, and she gulped, looked up at the tree and then across to him. Considered her options. If she refused it would be awkward. After all, she wouldn't give it a thought if someone else had suggested it.

'Fine. What's the best way to do it?'

Luca inhaled a deep breath. 'I'll squat down...' he suited action to word '...and you... hop on.'

This was the world's worst idea but if either of them acknowledged that it would mean they didn't have this attraction under control and she was damned if she'd admit that.

Before she could change her mind, she 'hopped on' and tried to ignore how that meant effectively wrapping her legs round his face. Tried not to notice the muscle of his shoulders, the easy grace with which he rose and balanced her weight.

Focus on the damn tree, Em. Pretend he is a chair, an inanimate object.

Not possible when she could sense the vital strength of him; he stood sturdy and strong, unbowed by her weight. His hands encircled her calves, his grip gentle but it steadied her, so she didn't sway. Calves were not a sensory part of one's body. They weren't. Or surely they weren't supposed to be. But her brain had clearly got it all mixed up because all she could feel was his hands on her, branding her.

Focus. On the tree, on the living, flourishing tree. Somehow Luca's touch, the warmth and strength of him, seemed to make the tree come alive to her eye. Made the green more vibrant, the bark softer to her gentle touch, every sense heightened because of him. As she looked at the pod ripe and full of life, inhaled the tang of the fruit, the delicate scent of the flower, her head whirled. But she knew it wasn't only the force of nature, it was something to do with Luca, and all she wanted was to slide down, feel the strength of his chest, stand toe to toe with him. To touch and hold and kiss him.

But she wouldn't, couldn't.

Aware that at some point she had stopped taking pictures, was simply balanced on him, she forced her voice to work. 'I'm done. Thank you.'

Slowly he lowered himself to the ground and she scrambled off with as much dignity as she could, turned to face him and suddenly realised how close he was, and her heightened senses soared.

The sound of someone clearing their throat caused them both to turn, the moment broken as a woman stepped forward, an apologetic smile on her face.

She started to speak, the Indian language of familiar cadence to Emily, but she had never learnt it and now it was her turn to smile apologetically as she shook her head and turned her hands up.

The woman pointed to the camera round Emily's neck and then at herself before putting her palms together and holding them up in a gesture that clearly indicated 'please'.

'Of course.' Emily smiled her understanding and took a few pictures of the smiling woman, including one with Luca.

With another beaming smile the woman left and Emily turned to Luca, relieved that the interlude had hopefully eradicated the previous atmosphere. 'I'll develop the photos and give them to Samar.' She glanced at her watch. 'We'd better head back for tea and cakes.'

Fifteen minutes later they sat in a cool white-walled room, decorated with family pictures, some clearly from a previous era, garlanded in fragrant chains of flowers. Samar had introduced his wife, Shamini, a slender petite woman with grey-streaked black hair and a serene smile.

'These are delicious,' Emily said as she bit into the sweet, crumbly round *laddu*.

'Thank you. I am pleased you like them.'

'Was your tour successful?' Samar questioned.

'Definitely,' Emily said, and sudden heat touched her cheeks at a memory of being astride Luca's shoulders. 'We met one of your employees, a woman called Priya. She asked for a photograph of her and Luca. I'll get it developed and send it to you for her if that's OK.'

'Of course.' Samar nodded. 'I too have a request. If you have time whilst you are here and Luca can spare you, would you perhaps take on an additional job, take some photos of the farm for our website?'

Emily hesitated, glanced down at her plate, picked up her cup of tea and put it down again as doubts pervaded. 'Um…to be honest that isn't my speciality. The pictures I took today are more for inspiration and ideas for Luca's ad campaign and…' And in truth she didn't want to do it, could see Howard's slow head-shake, the incredulous rise of an eyebrow that she was even considering it. It was one thing suggesting a few pictures of Luca for a website, but this was…an actual job. Plus Luca hadn't taken her up on her offer—true, he'd explained why but… somehow insidious doubt crept in and there was Howard's voice now. *Stick to what you know.*

Countered, she realised, by the very real and present voice of Luca. 'That sounds right up your street, Emily.' He turned to the couple. 'Emily took some wonderful photos already and earlier today she came up with some amazing ideas for my website. I think she'll do a great job.'

Now she was torn, between her inner doubts and pleasure at the endorsement. 'Of course, I'd like to help,' she said.

'Excellent.'

Now Shamini beamed at her. 'And I too have a request. Would you be able to take a family portrait for us to put on our wall? We have four children and eight grandchildren and we have no picture of us all.'

'No problem.' That she could do.

'Thank you. We will, of course, pay you.'

Emily shook her head. 'For the website pictures, sure, but I will not accept payment for the family photo. I feel like you have paid me in cakes.'

'I can go one better than that.' Shamini clapped her hands together. 'You and Luca come with Samar and me to the local dance tonight. There is a performance by a visiting dance troupe and then it becomes a bit of a party.'

'Um…' Emily exchanged a quick glance with Luca, read in his gaze that, not only would it be impolite to refuse, but an evening in company would be much safer than a dinner *à deux*. A whole village would surely act as an effective chaperone. 'That sounds marvellous.' She took a deep breath. 'Would it be OK if I got started on the website pictures now?'

'Good idea,' Samar said. 'As long as Luca can spare you?'

Luca rose to his feet. 'No problem. I'll meet

you back at the resort and we can walk down to the dance, grab some food on the way.'

Later that evening, Luca looked up as Emily approached the entrance to the resort, noted the lithe grace of her walk, and to his own chagrin his heart pitter-pattered at the sight of a woman he had seen mere hours before.

'How was your day?'

They asked the question at the same time and she smiled, a smile that stopped him in his tracks. 'You go first,' she said.

Luca hesitated. In truth he'd spent his afternoon looking for clues as to what Jodi had done whilst on Jalpura. He'd secured a meeting with Pradesh Patankar, the royal representative, in two days' time. The exchange of emails had been brief and to the point and all related to Luca's request to apply for royal endorsement of his chocolate. There was no indication from Pradesh that the Petrovelli name was familiar, but perhaps that meant nothing. Perhaps the royal representative had simply assumed it was a common name, or a coincidence. Next Luca had gone to the hostel where Jodi had stayed, followed up his previous calls, but he'd drawn a complete blank. The proprietor thought he had a vague memory of Jodi, but given the volume of visitors he couldn't even be sure of that.

'Luca?'

He heard the concern in Emily's voice and blinked, erased the frown from his forehead. 'Sorry. I was thinking about work. I caught up with the office. And I have a meeting set up with the royal representative to discuss the endorsement.'

'That's brilliant.' Her smile of approbation deepened the sense of wrongness at not sharing the whole truth. And for a moment he was tempted to do just that, explain about Jodi, tell Emily of his worry for his sister. But that was the point, he wouldn't only be sharing his worries, he'd be sharing Jodi's business in the sure knowledge that Jodi would see that as a betrayal. Hell, Jodi would be mad enough that Luca was here on Jalpura, let alone if he involved Ava's best friend in his capers.

'How was *your* day?'

'I took some shots for Samar's website.'

He heard the flatness in her voice and frowned. 'You don't sound happy.'

She shrugged. 'I'm not. If I'm honest I kind of wish I hadn't agreed or that...'

'Or that I didn't push you into it?' he asked, and she nodded.

'I'm sure you meant well but...' He heard doubt as to his motives and he frowned.

'I did mean well—you have taken so many

pictures since we've been here and I've seen how much energy you put into them, how enthusiastic you are. I thought this was an opportunity for you. To try something different.'

'I told you already that I don't want or need to do that.'

He decided to try a different tack, still didn't understand why she wouldn't follow her dream. 'Can I see the pictures?'

'Um…sure…at some point… I guess. I haven't had a chance to look at them, pick out the best ones, and you'd only be able to see them on a screen right now, which isn't the same as—'

'So you could show me them on your phone now.'

'Well, yes. I can access them from my phone but…'

There was genuine discomfort in her stance now, her shoulders had drooped and one arm crossed her waist, her gaze averted from his, and he came to a halt, oblivious to the people who thronged round them.

Glancing round, he spotted a small low-walled courtyard and he made his way over and perched on the stone ledge. Reluctantly she followed, and he risked a smile. 'That's the first time I've understood the phrase dragging your feet,' he observed. 'What on earth is wrong?'

'Nothing.'

Luca watched as she sat on the wall; her expression showed a worry that verged on fear and he frowned. Perhaps he should back off but this didn't make sense, plus it occurred to him, 'Ever since we got to Turin you must have taken hundreds of pictures but you haven't shown me a single one. Apart from one of me.'

'You haven't asked,' she countered, and then bit her lip as she realised the opening she'd given him.

One he instantly took. 'I'm asking now.'

'I'd rather show you the finished products. It makes more sense.'

'I can just about see that if it's for the ad campaign, but why can't you show me the pictures of the cocoa farm? I'm interested.'

'I can.' Emily sighed. 'Of course, I can.' But he sensed the tension that still emanated from her body as she pulled out her phone and tapped a few buttons. 'Here you go.'

She handed him the phone, and turned away, arms folded across her middle.

This really didn't make sense; he'd expected her to want to show them to him, had looked forward to her enthusiasm, the gestures, the smile. If he were completely honest he would have welcomed the closeness, the tickle of her hair as she leant over to point something out.

Now he remembered her trepidation in the London café, but that had been when she was touting for the job. Then he had understood her worries. But surely not now; why would she fear his judgement now? Yet he could see doubt and fear in her brown eyes and in the tap of her foot and the slump of her shoulders.

He looked down at her phone; her fear was infectious and for a mad instant he was sure he'd see a mishmash of out-of-focus images on the screen. He studied the first photograph, a glorious picture of a woman next to a cocoa tree, reaching up to check one of the ripe pods. The woman wasn't young yet her body, the slightly calloused tips to her fingers, showed the suppleness of a woman used to hard work. Somehow the wide smile on her face, the vivid colours of her sari, the browns and verdant colours of the trees, the intense blue of the sky, all combined to show joy in her work, and in the beauty of her surroundings.

Luca continued to scroll down, marvelled at how Emily had captured the essence of the farm, beauty combined with a place of work, growth and productivity. The lush ripeness of the pods, the sheer quirkiness of the coconuts, the wave of the tree fronds, the movement of people going about their tasks, the casual intimacy of two women laughing as they worked, the concentration on the face of a young man pruning a tree.

He turned to her, saw she hadn't moved, her stillness rigid as if she braced herself for his verdict.

'These are absolutely bloody brilliant,' he said. 'You've brought the farm to life for everyone to see. As an overview and in the detail. I can almost smell the trees, feel the sun on my face. I want to meet these people.'

Very slowly she relaxed, and he was rewarded with a tentative upturn of her lips, though her eyes still held scepticism, her frown one of disbelief. 'You don't have to be nice.'

'I'm not being nice. I'm being truthful.' He studied her expression. 'Surely you can see how good they are.'

'Honestly? No, I can't. All I can see is what I may have done wrong, wrong perspective, angle, feel, colour… I'm terrified to show them to Samar. I don't even want to show you anything I've done for the campaign. I think I'm just all ideas—all snap-snap-snap, all mouth and no follow through.'

Their conversation on the plane came back to him, her conviction that her metier was fashion photography and she didn't have the talent or ability to move into a different sphere.

'Look, I know I am not an expert, but I don't

need to be—I am the target audience. I promise those photos will appeal to anyone looking at Samar's website. But I believe they are
worth more even that that—I think you could
do a photo documentary on Jalpura. On the life
on this island. You said yourself it is a fascinating place—an independent Indian island with
a royal family.'

'I told you—'

'I know what you told me, and I profoundly
disagree.' He eyed her closely. 'What expert told
you that you don't have what it takes?'

She hesitated, then, 'Howard.'

For one incredulous moment he stared at her.
'Your ex-husband.'

'Yes.' Her eyes narrowed at his expression.
'But he wasn't my ex when he told me. It's how
we met—he agreed to do a critique, an assess-
ment of my work. He told me the truth. He
didn't have to—he could have strung me along
because he wanted to date me, but he didn't.
And the points made sense.'

'Perhaps he believed what he said, but that
doesn't mean he is right.'

Emily looked at him. 'He is a globally renowned photographer. He's won every award
there is.'

Luca waved his hand. 'That still doesn't
make him infallible and you can't trust that

his opinion wasn't coloured by his relationship with you.'

'I get that, and I spent months trying to prove him wrong. In the end I gave up my career to be his assistant because I hoped I'd learn from him.'

'And did you?'

'No.' Her voice was small now. 'He tried but it was frustrating for him. To be fair to him he genuinely saw fashion as an inferior branch of photography, something frothy and frivolous, so to him my work was…not very important.'

'But what you do is part of a billion-dollar industry.'

'Howard doesn't care about money. And I can't blame him for criticising my work. It was full of flaws, in my technique, the angles, the light. Sometimes he'd take a picture of the same thing I had and he'd point out the differences.'

Anger began to rise in Luca, but he kept his voice even. 'Just out of interest, did he ever say anything positive?'

'Of course.'

'Let me guess—it was always followed by a "but" or was a backhanded compliment.'

Luca forced himself not to rise and pace. 'It sounds like he wanted to undermine you, and it sounds to me like his voice is still in your head.'

'Of course, it isn't. Or at least not in a bad

way. I'd be a fool to discount his opinion on photography.'

'No, you wouldn't. I am not dissing Howard's talents, but I do think his perspective was warped by your relationship.' Plus the man sounded like a bully and he suspected Emily's marriage had been marred by a bullying she wasn't even aware of. Because she was so star-struck by the man's talent she believed his words to be gospel. But it explained her fear of showing her work, the way she expected criticism, the fact she still had Howard's words in her head. Just as the taunts of those schoolyard bullies had echoed in his.

'Perhaps.' Emily shrugged. 'It doesn't really matter.' She rose to her feet. 'Shall we walk?'

'Sure.' He followed suit, looked down at the sudden pinched look on her face and he knew it did matter, that he had to try and convince her that Howard was wrong. 'We can talk whilst we walk.'

CHAPTER ELEVEN

As they started to walk the thronged noisy streets, redolent with the scent of spices and rich with the sound of chatter, the honk of horns and the cries of street vendors hawking their wares, Emily considered Luca's words, wondered if he could be right. When she'd taken the pictures at the farm it had felt…'right'. As she'd snapped she'd felt in the zone, as if everything had come together.

It was only when it came to showing them to Luca that doubt had assailed her and she'd prepared herself to be put down. But that wasn't down to Luca, that was down to her—she'd grown to assume and believe negativity from Howard, not just on her work, but on everything. She had been sure during their marriage that he had become more and more judgemental because of her inability to learn from him. That that inability had made him see only her flaws and not the things that had presumably made him marry her in the first place.

But how could she question whether he was right? He was Howard McAllister.

Luca glanced down at her and his voice was quiet now, his grey eyes dark with purpose. 'Those photos are good, Emily. Don't let Howard's voice stay in your head telling you they aren't.'

'It's not that easy. If you went to your mentor and he said you only had the talent to produce mass chocolate what would you have done?'

'Gone away and produced the best mass-produced chocolate in the business and gone back to the drawing board. I'd have proved him wrong.' He shrugged. 'But there is a big difference here. My mentor is a gentleman. Yours sounds like a bully. And bullies have power. I don't think Howard's opinion of your work was unbiased.'

'You can't know that.'

'No, but I do know a bully when I see one. And I remember what it is like to be taunted and put down—not in the same context, but I know how much it can hurt. I am telling you this so you know what I am saying is not just empty words.'

Now she focused on him, saw the remembered hurt in his eyes and knew this was a trip down memory lane he didn't want to take.

'I told you that when my father left life was tough. But after a while my mother pulled us through the toughest bit, there was more money, I was settled in school, life became more normal. But then things began to change. As Dolci grew so did the publicity around the Casseveti name. A boy at my school figured out who I was and he latched onto it. Asked where my dad was, why I never saw him, told me my dad didn't love me because I was so weak, came up with different reasons and made me repeat them…and soon it caught on and then it escalated. Into relentless bullying.'

'That's awful.' Her heart cracked as she imagined the young Luca, a small boy having his vulnerabilities displayed and exploited; she could almost feel how much each taunt must have seared his soul. And to force him to list reasons why his dad had left took cruelty to a new level, was tantamount to Howard listing out all her faults and flaws and making her repeat them. At least he had stopped short of that. 'I'm sorry you had to go through that.'

He shook his head. 'I didn't tell you because I want your pity. I told you because I know what that treatment does to you. It undermines you and makes you insecure and miserable. It eats away at your soul and makes you crumble inside. It erodes your confidence and it can make you doubt everything about yourself. I endured it at school, you had to live with it. Howard forcing you to spot the difference, his constant putdowns, his dismissal of your achievements as frothy and frivolous. He is a grown-up version of the boy who made my life so miserable.'

His words made her pause. Of course, she knew Howard was a full-scale cheating rat, a man who had cheated on his pregnant wife, a man who had quite simply not given a flying fish for his unborn child. Yet because the man's photographic talent could not be questioned, she'd still accepted that all the put-downs, all the criticisms of her work were justified.

Just as she was sure Luca would have believed the awful cruel taunts of his persecutor. Would have believed his father's abandonment was his fault. The idea heated anger in her veins as well as compassion for the child he'd been.

'I hope that boy got what was coming to him, or at least some help. I hope he saw the error of his ways, but before he did I hope someone bopped him on the nose or something.'

His expression crinkled into amusement and she frowned. 'It's not funny.'

'I know it's not, but I guess we are both displaying a violent streak. I was just thinking how

I wish Howard were here so I could kick him round Jalpura.'

They both contemplated the idea and then she turned to him and without even realising it she slipped her hand into his. 'What happened?' she asked. 'With the bullying?'

'Nothing. I endured it. I was too ashamed to tell my mum. Things were finally going well for her. She'd qualified as a lawyer, she'd even started another relationship. And I didn't want to tell her. I was meant to be the...' He broke off and she completed the sentence.

'The man of the family.' And her heart cracked a little more even as anger surged at James Casseveti for leaving his son so heartlessly.

'Yes,' he acknowledged. 'And to be frank the whole situation was far from manly. I couldn't tell anyone, so I endured it. Until one day I snapped. They decided to take it a step further; they brought my mother into it, started trying to make me say filth about her. I saw red. I went for the leader. I'd love to say I won but I didn't. But he did get bopped on the nose— my only satisfaction is that I did get in a good few punches and kicks and I certainly surprised him. But he was bigger than me and had a couple of friends there too. The teachers pulled us apart and obviously after that adults were involved. I didn't tell the whole of it, but other kids were questioned and they did. I wish they hadn't.'

'Why?'

'Because it made me feel weak. As though I needed to be looked after.'

'You did need to be looked after. You were a child.'

'I get that, but it didn't feel like that back then. It felt humiliating and as if I'd let my mum down. That's what bullying does to you—it makes you lose perspective.'

'So what did your mum do?'

'She let rip at the school, and before I knew it she had pulled me out of school and decided we were moving to Italy, that we were changing our name to her maiden name, Petrovelli.'

'So that was why you had a new start.'

'That's why. Mum's new relationship didn't work out, but she said it didn't matter because she fell in love with Italy instead. We all did. So it all worked out.'

Suddenly he halted and turned so they faced each other, took her other hand in his as well. 'I'd like it to work out for you too. Don't let Howard ruin your chance to do something you want to do with your photography. Don't believe his words.'

'It's not that easy.'

'I know,' he said softly, and she wondered if he still believed the words of those bullies so long ago. Still believed it was his fault his father had left. 'But you can try.'

Emily took a deep breath. 'OK. I'll try. I'll think about the idea of a Jalpura documentary.' For a long moment they stood, hands linked, and a strange trickle of warmth, of hope, of lightness ran through her. Until finally the hustle and bustle of people urged them to keep walking and Luca pointed to a nearby food stall.

'Shall we try that one? I am suddenly ravenous. And we need to eat before the dance.'

'Me too. That one sounds perfect.' And as he tugged her towards the enticing aroma she realised she was smiling.

Luca swallowed the last delicious mouthful of *biriani* and they started to walk towards the temple where the dance was going to take place.

'I am very excited about this,' Emily said. 'I've always wanted to see Kathakali performed.'

'Kathakali?'

'Yes, Samar and Shamini mentioned it earlier, after you'd gone. My dad told me about it. It's a dance that tells a story. It literally means story play. The dancers have years and years of training because it's so hard. The whole story is conveyed through gesture and facial expression and colour. The make-up is exquisite and basically different colours represent different characters and characteristics. It's amazingly complex and the story is usually epic. The performances can go on throughout the night.' She glanced up at him and gave a gurgle of laughter. 'Not today, though. Today is one scene from the story of Nala and Damayanti. It's a love story, but they have a pretty torturous path with demons and battles and magic and snakes before they get their happy ending.'

She broke off. 'Sorry. I am boring on.'

'Nope. You aren't.' He grinned at her. 'I think you'd have made a natural Kathakali dancer.'

'Hah. Just because I move my hands around a bit when I talk.'

'There's that, but it's also the way your nose crinkles when you dislike something and the crease on your forehead when you are focusing.' He studied each feature and his fingers tingled with a desire to smooth his fingers against her brow, to move down the bridge of her nose. 'Then there's your smile.'

He heard her intake of breath at his words, a sound she turned into a shaky laugh. 'I think you need more than a few wrinkles to be a Kathakali dancer.'

As she spoke they reached their destination, saw Samar and Shamini waiting for them, and now they turned their attention to the performance.

'Part of the whole experience is to watch the dancers transform,' Samar explained, and they watched a dancer lie prostrate as other members of the troupe applied a complicated *maquillage*. 'He is the main dancer, he is Nala, so he has the most complicated make-up.'

A few minutes later the performance began, the dancers assembled around a large multi-wicked bell metal lamp. Bare-chested musicians encircled the actors, drums to hand.

Luca's eyes widened as he witnessed the intricacies, the grace, the drama, the wealth of detailed movement that told the story. The scene showed Nala finally defeated by an evil demon who poisoned his character, made him into a gambler who wagered away his kingdom and deserted his wife. Perhaps that was what had happened to his father, Luca thought; his Achilles heel, his greed, had been exploited by a demon woman who would stop at nothing to get him.

Emily's words of earlier rang through his head. *'The very act of living your life as you have, of being a true family with your mum and Jodi, all you have achieved despite what he did*

*to you all—that is success and you mustn't let
anything take that away from you.'*

He turned to look at her as she stared wide-
eyed and rapt at the stage; he'd swear he saw
the suspicion of tears in her eyes as she swayed
to the evocative beat of the drums, as the wife
Damayanti wept as Nala crept into the night.

Looking down, he saw that at some stage in
the proceedings he'd taken her hand in his. For a
moment he considered releasing his grip, knew
he didn't want to, told himself that it was all to
do with the atmosphere, the beat of the drum,
the flare of the fires that had sprung up throughout the grounds.

The applause was long and soon after the
performers melted away. 'Now it's over to us,'
Shamini said. 'I think we should dance the *kol-
kali.*'

They watched as groups of men and women
formed circles; from somewhere came a sup-
ply of sticks that were passed around and both
he and Emily gripped them. Other people held
instruments, drums and cymbals. Luca looked
to Emily for elucidation but she shrugged her
shoulders. 'I have no idea how to do this.' Worry
clouded her eyes as she looked down at the stick
and Luca wanted to dispel it.

'Then let's just go with it,' he said, and a sudden exhilaration raced through him as he held

out a hand to her. 'Together.' Because he wanted to dance with her, wanted her to abandon herself to the sound of the drums as she had for scant seconds back in Silvio's in Turin. Perhaps it would give her a release from the doubts and sadness he knew she carried, would lighten the load.

Surprise lit her eyes along with a second of hesitation and then she tucked a strand of hair behind her ear and placed her hand in his with a shy smile. 'Let's do it.'

The feel of her hand in his again brought a smile to his face and he squeezed it slightly, caught his breath as she moved closer to him, and he felt intoxicated by her proximity, her scent, her warmth.

Within minutes the music started, the beat slow at first, and the group began to move in a circle striking the sticks against each other, whilst keeping rhythm with different steps. Luca released Emily's hand but stayed close as they both tried to follow along, and soon enough they were swept up in the rhythm. Yet Luca was only aware of Emily, the rest of the crowd a mere backdrop against this entrancing woman, the sway and curve of her body, the grace of her movements and the expression on her face, her eyes focused on him.

The music increased in tempo and volume,

and the movements became faster and faster as the circle of dancers expanded and contracted, the sticks a blur in the moonlight, and through it all Emily weaved and turned, the dance bringing her so tantalisingly close and then pulling her away, and it seemed to him that they danced for each other and each other alone.

Then another dancer tripped, lost his balance and stumbled into Emily's path; she tried to dodge but her body twisted at an awkward angle and instantly Luca moved to catch her and then there she was in his arms. 'Are you OK?'

'I think so. Yes. Thank you.' Her voice was breathless as she looked up at him and now his chest constricted at her beauty, dark hair wild around her flushed face, her brown eyes warm and alive with laughter and passion, and now he knew that she had danced for him, had been as caught in the spell as he was. Knew too he should let her go but instead his arms tightened around her as he told himself she might be hurt, might need his support. For a timeless instant they stood, and his head whirled as he saw desire spark in her eyes, her lips parted, and he couldn't help himself. Oblivious to the dancers around them, he lowered his head and kissed her.

CHAPTER TWELVE

THE TOUCH OF Luca's lips blew Emily's mind, cascaded her with feeling, made her feel alive for the first time in such a long, long time and she gave in to it. To the sheer raw visceral passion his lips aroused in her. She revelled in it as he deepened the kiss and wrapped his hands in her hair so that she let out a small moan of sheer unadulterated pleasure, pressed harder against him, wanting more. Wanting the barriers of the soft cotton T-shirt to be gone. Pleasure and frustration vied inside her in a whirling, squirming, hot mess of desire.

Until she knew she couldn't take any more. 'We need to go,' she said.

He nodded. There was no need for words, their sole focus now on assuaging the churn of need. All thoughts of one moment in time gone, discarded, abandoned without question. She was no longer capable of rational thought, her whole being motivated by desire for this man.

'We need to find Samar and Shamini.'

Luca dropped a curse but then nodded and somehow they got through the goodbyes, the necessary chit-chat, and then they were half walking, half running back to the resort. All that mattered now was getting to the hotel. A journey achieved in near silence, though his hand remained firmly clasped around hers. Almost as though, if they broke the link, common sense would weasel its way back in, and she gripped his fingers with equal fervour. Every so often he would brush his lips against hers and anticipation surged through her until her head whirled.

Then finally—finally—they got to the hotel and she followed him blindly to his thatched cottage, simply because it was nearest. He closed the door, moved to the windows and pulled the blinds down so the room was cocooned in cool dusky darkness.

For one fleeting moment a sudden panic touched her, a wonder if her body could do this, could remember how. Whether after the ordeal she'd been through she could expose herself. One hand smoothed over her now flat stomach and a pang of sadness touched her.

As if he sensed her change he stilled, slowed down and she looked up at him, his face shadowed now, but she could see concern dawn in his eyes. 'We don't have to do this, Emily. If you've changed your mind, that's fine.'

Had she? Or could she allow herself this? Set aside grief for a short while. He watched her, his gaze steady and full of reassurance, and she knew if she backed off he would fall in with her wishes without recrimination and with a level of understanding. His concern added a new layer of sweetness, and a different kind of warmth touched her senses. 'I haven't changed my mind.'

And this time the kiss was different, soft and sweet and almost tentative and it felt, oh, so completely right, and now as they walked backwards towards the bed and he lowered her gently down she smiled at him. Knew in that moment that she was in safe hands and she reached up to tug him down next to her. Then all doubts vanished as his lips covered hers and with tantalising slowness and exquisite promise he unbuttoned the front of her dress.

Then all thought stopped and she lost herself in the vortex of need and want, of laughter and pleasure; the feel of skin on skin, the touch of his fingers, the sweep of his back, the scent of citrus and bergamot and Luca all assailed her senses.

Luca opened his eyes, instantly aware of Emily in the crook of his arm, and he made sure to remain still, wanted to let her sleep. As he looked at her, eyes closed, the curve of her eyelashes against her cheek, the silken tangle of her hair, a strange sense of wonder shivered through him. He lay back and stared up at the white of the ceiling, heard the sound of a bird from outside and luxuriated in the sheer magic of this moment.

On that thought she opened her eyes and he watched, revelled in the sheer intimacy of watching. Her small puzzled frown, her lazy smile as memory dawned and then she rolled away from him, sat bolt upright, sheet clutched to her chest.

'Oh…' she said. 'It really happened.'

'It really did.' He couldn't help but smile and she smiled back, a small shy smile but a smile none the less and, encouraged, he wriggled up the headboard so he was next to her, side by side, their legs pressed together in the warm aftermath of intimacy. Perhaps he should feel regret for the previous night but he didn't, perhaps he should also feel worry or concern about the next steps but right now he couldn't muster up the energy.

'I don't know what to say,' she said finally. 'I really don't. I mean, this is exactly what we were trying to avoid but…'

'It's a bit difficult right now to figure out why.'

'That's for sure.' There was a silence and then she tucked the sheet more securely round herself, moved even closer to him. 'I do have an idea.'

'Go ahead.'

'We both know this can't go anywhere. I don't want your type of relationship and you don't want mine. In truth right now I am too hurt to even contemplate a relationship anyway. But last night was…'

'Magical, amazing, glorious…'

Now she laughed, a small gurgle of a chuckle. 'All of those things. And I don't really see the point in shutting the stable door after the horse has bolted.'

'So you are suggesting we stay in the stable and bolt it from the inside?'

'Something like that. I'm saying that whilst we are here on Jalpura we should keep doing…' she gestured over the bed '…this. Maybe see this as a bubble in time. I'd like that—a bubble where I can insulate myself from the real world.' For a second, sadness flitted across her face and he wondered what secrets she still held to her.

'A time to just experience the moment?' he asked.

'Yes. And once we go home it all comes to a natural end. I'll deal with your marketing team then anyway, so our paths don't even need to cross. But *now* is a time to be happy and enjoy what's on offer.' Now she turned slightly so she was looking into his eyes. 'And I do understand what is on offer. Nothing heavy. All your usual caveats are in place. No expectations, no clinginess. Low-key, not intense. Fun and easy.'

Luca recognised his own words and a qualm hit him; was that what he wanted with Emily? The question jolted him with panic and he focused on keeping his expression neutral as she continued to speak.

'I know I don't match a lot of your other criteria.' He couldn't help his slight flinch—somehow the idea of criteria didn't seem as... valid...as it had a few nights ago. 'But that's OK, because this is a strictly short-term arrangement. I guess you'll have to think of me as an anomaly.'

More qualms hit him—this was breaking all his rules and he was suddenly scared he couldn't handle it, because his thoughts were spinning out of control. She was so near, so beautiful, so... Emily and he was scared that he'd let her too close.

'If that works for you?' Her voice went small and he knew that she feared rejection, could read his doubts.

Chill, Luca.

This was an overreaction. Because the bottom line was that he and Emily wanted different things—she did not want a long-term arrangement on his terms, she wanted a husband and a family and that was a no-go area for him. So she was right. This was a bubble, a blip if you will, and if Emily wanted fun and joy and magic then that was what he would provide.

'It completely works for me. You are a beautiful, magical anomaly,' he said and was rewarded with a smile. 'As long as you are sure this…' and now he gestured around '…is what you want.'

'I'm sure.' Her voice held certainty, and he saw nothing in her eyes to cast doubt on her word, though he still sensed a vulnerability, a fragility to her desire for a few days of happiness. And in that moment he vowed he would do all in his power to give her that; there could be no harm in that.

'Then how about we start right now with a little bit of this?' With a big grin on his face he tugged at the sheet, was rewarded by a small shriek from Emily as she reached for it.

'Hey, give that back.'

Now his grin broadened. 'Make me.'

With a breathless laugh she lunged for it and he moved beneath her, caught her into an embrace, so she sat astride him, looking down, her glorious hair loose, the tips tickling his chest.

Then she leaned down and kissed him and the sheet dropped from his hand forgotten as he kissed her right back.

An hour later they lay entwined and tangled in the sheets and Luca marvelled at how he and Emily had come to this. No rules, no regulations and right now he didn't care, because this felt like the most natural thing in the world.

He dropped a kiss on the top of her head, revelled in the feel of her silken hair. 'So what's the plan for the day?'

'Breakfast. I am ravenous. Then later today I'm going to take the family picture for Shamini and then I thought we'd stick to plan. Go for a walk and see the sunset at the summit—I think it may be a good location for the shoot?'

'Sounds like a plan.'

She rolled a little away from him and propped herself up on her elbow. 'Also I thought we could go through some photos. If you like. To take with you to your meeting with the royal representative.' Her smile was a little shy and he could sense the sudden tension in her body. 'I thought you could show them to him and suggest a quid pro quo. They endorse your chocolate and we'll make sure Jalpura is advertised as an amazing tourist destination as part of the campaign.'

Luca sat up, leaned against the headboard and she followed suit. As he put an arm around her shoulders a conflict of emotions coursed through him. 'Thank you.' He knew how hard it was for her to show off her work, knew how much the offer meant. 'That is an excellent idea.' But alongside pride in Emily was discomfort at his own actions. After all, his main goal of the meeting was to find out information about Jodi. Luca hesitated, his brain whirring—surely he could trust her to keep Jodi's situation confidential...surely it couldn't harm to share some information? But if he did that Emily would ask questions...and who knew what she'd find out? And it wasn't his business to share. Yet it felt wrong to lie, even if the lie was only one of omission. Especially when she was willing to go so far out of her own comfort zone to help him.

Before he could decide her phone rang; she picked it up from the bedside drawer and glanced down, then back up at him. 'It's Ava. It's probably her daily check-in, about the wedding plans.'

The words pulled him back to reality—saved by the bell. Emily was Ava's best friend, the reminder one he shouldn't even need. Quickly he moved away, swung his legs over the side of the bed. 'I'll go and sort out some breakfast. You talk to Ava,' he said.

'OK.' A pause, then she said his name and he turned to face her. 'I won't tell Ava about us. This is between you and me. There is no need for her to know.'

'Agreed.' Her words, a reassurance, tipped the scales towards the possibility of confidence. 'I won't be long.'

She nodded. 'Cool. Thank you.'

He returned half an hour later, pushed a trolley through the door. In his absence she'd pulled on one of his T-shirts and was curled up in one of the wicker chairs. For a moment he wondered if he should ask about Ava, decided to avoid it. Somehow the idea that she was keeping them a secret made him feel a little uncomfortable. A reminder of why he'd vowed not to get involved with Emily. But that ship had sailed and he couldn't bring himself to regret it.

He gestured to the bed. 'I thought we'd have breakfast in bed?'

Her eyes widened as she surveyed the laden trolley.

'*Dosas*, *idlis*, vegetable curry with egg, and masala potatoes and, of course, some coffee.' All her favourites.

'We can't eat that in bed. We'll make a mess.'

'That's the fun of it,' he said. 'We can get as messy...' and now he smiled at her '...or as dirty as we want.' He wiggled his eyebrows and she gave a low, sweet laugh.

'I'm in.'

And soon they were back in the bed, plates on their knees.

'This feels ridiculously decadent,' she said. 'We should be working…'

'Work-schmerk. We'll get plenty of that done later. Right now you need to taste this.' Carefully he scooped up some potatoes in a piece of *dosa* and obediently she opened her mouth so he could pop it in.

'My God, that is incredible.' She closed her eyes and he watched as she savoured the taste, felt a warmth of intimacy as they continued to eat, fed each other pieces of fruit until they were replete.

'I don't think I'll ever eat again,' she said. 'Or at least till lunchtime.'

There was a pause and then she took a deep breath, glanced sideways at him. 'Ava said to say hi.'

Luca realised he had no idea what to say. He settled for, 'Say hi back.'

'Also, Ava asked me to ask you something. She doesn't want to put you on the spot by asking herself. I don't want to wait to tell you so…'

'Go ahead.' Foreboding touched him.

'Would you walk her down the aisle at her wedding?'

The question came from nowhere and he knew the shock must show on his face.

'She knows it is a big ask but she just wants you to think about it. You don't have to answer now.'

'I can answer now. I don't think that would work.' The idea of taking on the role that James Casseveti would have done with such pride and joy and love seemed impossible to even contemplate, brought a complex swirl of emotion to the surface. He swung himself out of bed, pulled on his chinos and started to pace. 'I am surprised Ava would even want that.'

Emily joined him, dressed in his T-shirt that fell to below her knees; she placed a hand on his arm. 'You're her brother. Her family.'

'No.' Luca closed his eyes, then opened them again. 'Ava's life and mine have been carried out separately and apart—we are only "family" because we chance to share a "father". It is blood, not family. Family is about the bond you feel with people you grow up with and care about and who care for you. I like Ava but I can't make her into real family.' He saw a flash of sadness cross her face. 'I'm sorry.'

Emily shook her head. 'But you could get to know her, forge a bond with her. Of course, it would be different from your bond with your mother and Jodi, but it would still be real.'

'There is too much history between us.' He kept his voice gentle. 'I know it is not Ava's fault what her father, our father did. But it will always be there.' The knowledge that she had been chosen over him, had kept James Casseveti's love in a way Luca hadn't. That was his real failure and he had no need of any reminders.

'I understand that. But I still think you should try, otherwise your father's actions are still affecting the present, preventing you and Ava from developing a relationship.' She stepped forward and now her brown eyes held a plea. 'You have a choice. I get it would be hard but…'

Anger flickered into being; how could Emily get it? 'That is easy to say.'

Reading his expression, she reached out and took his hand, the touch warm and sweet, and it soothed the anger as she led him over to the wicker sofa. They sat down, still hand in hand. 'I *do* get it. I get how hard it is to accept the favoured child, the one who actually grows up with a parent, sees them every day, is part of their real family.'

Her words were sincere and he studied her face, saw genuine empathy there, and the penny dropped. Emily had spoken of her dad's second family, the brood of children. 'You speak of your father's second family?'

'Yes.'

'That is different. You have known those half-siblings all their life. You have a relationship with your dad.'

'Yes. But it is dilute, a shadow of what he has with my half-siblings. Don't get me wrong—he is fond of me. But I come second, I am of less importance. That's natural—he sees me twice a year, for a week at a time. He lives with his other kids, is there for all the milestones. I get I'm lucky he saw me at all, but growing up it affected how I feel about my siblings. Part of me resented them, even though I know it's not their fault.'

No, it had been her father's fault. Perhaps he could have done things differently, made an effort to see Emily on his own, made some time for her to forge their own separate bond. And now another penny clanged down. That was exactly what Emily was asking him to do now with Ava. He put that thought aside for the moment, wanting to know more about Emily.

'Do you still visit your family now?'

'I haven't for a while. In a way it still feels now how it did then. I wasn't part of their unit and I couldn't figure out how to infiltrate it. I was surplus to requirements.'

'So you watched from the sidelines?'

'Yes.'

'*I* get *that*.' He could picture a younger Emily, dark eyes wide and serious, at a busy bustling dinner table, listening to family 'jokes' she didn't understand, trying to work out what to say or do, how to get her dad's attention. And it sent a jolt of pain to his chest. 'I used to read all the celebrity magazines that followed Ava's lifestyle; I watched from the sidelines as well.' He'd studied the pictures with such intensity, looking for clues, hoping he'd see something in his father's expression that showed he felt regret, but all he'd seen was a father's love for his daughter.

'I'm sorry. That must have been difficult, to have to see and watch. At least I was part of my father's life.' She shook her head. 'I used to take photos of them all. It gave me something to do and later on I'd study them, try to work out what to do. Maybe if I did my hair like my younger sister, if I started to like superhero comics like my brother, would it help?'

'Did it?'

'Nope. In the end I figured it was best to stay invisible. And now it is all too late. They are still all a unit. They still have each other and they still don't need me. I have tried, truly I have, but I still can't figure out how. The bottom line is that they aren't really interested in me. That is their choice.'

'Maybe that will change, perhaps it's not too late—to forge some sort of bond. For you,' he added hastily.

'Then why is it too late for you? I know you don't need to. You and Jodi have each other, are a unit. But maybe you and Ava could form some kind of bond.'

'I don't think I can.' He heard the sadness in his own voice. 'There *is* too much history between Ava and me, even if we only met recently. Too much of that history is still with us. Ava loved her dad, loved and respected a man who tore my mother's life apart and deserted his children. There is no getting past that fact.'

'Not unless you want to,' Emily said softly. 'Unless you make the choice to try.' As her siblings hadn't. 'Because otherwise Ava is being punished for something she didn't do. And so are you. Missing out on getting to know someone who is your family by blood.'

As her siblings were missing out on a chance to know this woman.

'Look, please think about it. Not walking her down the aisle, but maybe just meeting up for a cup of coffee next time you are in London.'

'I'll think about it.'

'Good.' Her smile was so sweet and full of

satisfaction that he couldn't help but smile back and then her smile widened. 'And now I think reality has intruded enough. I think we should go back to bed.' Now *she* wiggled her eyebrows. 'We've been messy. Now let's get dirty.' The words were said with an exaggerated huskiness, and without further ado he rose and pulled her to her feet and swept her up in his arms and carried her to the bed.

CHAPTER THIRTEEN

LATER THAT DAY Emily glanced across at Luca as a car drove them out to the cocoa-bean farm, felt a sense of replete satisfaction mixed with the surreal. As she studied the strength of his face, his sculpted body, the shape of his hands she gave a small shiver of remembered pleasure. He turned his head and she saw his eyes darken, knew he could read her expression. Though that was hardly surprising; there was every chance she was drooling.

The car pulled to a stop and they climbed out with a quick thank you to the driver and headed towards the house. Emily smiled as Shamini pulled the door open with a welcoming smile. 'Come in. We are so happy you are doing this for us.'

Emily clocked the quick glance the older woman darted between her and Luca and wondered if she'd seen the kiss at the dance. 'So where would you like the photograph to be taken?' she said hurriedly.

'Let me make you a cup of tea and I'll explain my ideas. Luca, you can head to the lounge, where the family is gathering.'

As they headed into the cool interior a small girl hurtled towards Shamini and wrapped her arms around her legs in a hug. 'This is my granddaughter, Amelia,' she said. The girl peeped up shyly and then hid her face in the folds of Shamini's brightly coloured sari.

Emily glanced round the whitewashed kitchen, with its stone worktops and swept tiled floor and the lingering scent of spice in the air. Pans hung from the ceiling and she glimpsed a larder with jars full of rice and dried lentils and herbs.

Once tea was made she followed Shamini and Amelia into a large lounge.

'I think the photo should be in here, as it is here we have most space.'

Emily blinked—she knew that Samar and Shamini had four children and eight grandchildren, but knowing and seeing were two different things. The room was a hubbub of noise and children, a bright swirl of saris and western dress. Until Samar spotted them, picked up a bell and rang it loudly.

The noise levels subsided and everyone turned to the doorway.

'This is Emily, who has very kindly agreed

to take our picture. Emily, what would you like us to do? We're still waiting for my youngest daughter and her family, but we can get started.'

About ten minutes later Emily had sorted people out into a group and figured out lighting and backdrops, moved various things around and taken a few informal shots to warm everyone up.

The peal of the doorbell indicated the arrival of the final participants and minutes later a young couple walked in. 'I am so sorry we are late. Amitabh needed a nappy-change just when we were ready to leave,' the dark-haired woman said.

Emily saw now that the man held a baby in his arms and Shamini swept forward and took the baby, presented him proudly to Emily.

'The latest addition to the family.'

Emily gazed at the baby and from nowhere grief screamed towards her, hit her so hard that she almost stepped back. This was what her baby would have looked like. Her baby who had kicked inside her, the baby she had wanted so badly, had already loved so much.

'He's beautiful. How old is he?' Her voice was slightly strangled and she sensed Luca glance at her.

'Ten months. He started to crawl a few weeks ago.' The baby gurgled and then tilted forward, arms outstretched towards Emily. 'He likes you.' Shamini held the baby out and Emily could feel her body temperature plunge. Her skin felt clammy with a sudden sheen of panic and the reek of sadness, all the worse because it was so unexpected, had pelted in out of nowhere and struck.

Would her baby have started to crawl yet, weighed the same as this little one, would he too have had a shock of black hair or would his head have been downy with little wisps? The baby regarded her with immense solemnity and then grabbed her finger and started to chew it. A tsunami of grief swept through her as she held this warm, living miracle of existence in her arms. Sorrow underlaid with anger. Why had it happened to her? And guilt. What had she done wrong?

A part of her wanted to hold onto this baby and turn and run, go somewhere where the baby was hers, where the world had been different, where she could simply have the future she'd envisioned, with her child.

Then all of a sudden Luca was by her side; his sheer strength and bulk, full of reassurance, pulled her back to reality. His gaze rested on her, concern and care evident.

For one brief moment she allowed herself to breathe in the baby smell and then she gathered a smile together as she carefully handed Amitabh back to his mum, then turned away, pushed down the grief into the expanse of ache inside her.

'Right.' Picking up her camera, she said, 'Let's get this show on the road.'

And soon she looked through the lens at the grouped ensemble, this family standing together, a family who lived together clearly in harmony and friendship and love.

The knowledge that this couldn't happen for her clogged her throat, and she focused on the welcome familiarity of the camera's cold touch in her hand, channelled her everything into this. Perhaps she couldn't have it but she wouldn't grudge it to this family and she would do her best to provide them with a picture they could cherish, a picture that showed their bond, their connection and their love. In the way the grandmother held her granddaughter's hand, in the pride of a father in his children, in a wife's look of love to her husband and the respect and affection to her mother-in-law.

Once done, she found it in herself to mingle, chat to everyone, play with the children, all with a smile on her face. And through it all she was aware of Luca's gaze on her, the question and concern in his eyes, aware too that he was making this easier for her, just through his presence, the way he deflected conversation, the knowledge that she could lean against his strength if need be.

Whoa. No leaning, remember? No clinginess or emotional need. That was the deal— Luca had no wish to be exposed to another's pain or vulnerabilities. However understanding he'd already proven to be, this all ended in a few days. So she mustn't let herself get close on any other level.

Finally it was time to leave, to start their trek to the summit of a local mountain to see the sunset, check out the place as a possible photo shoot. Goodbyes said, they left the house, turned to wave at the family grouped outside and headed for the car.

'What's wrong?' Once they were in the cool of the air-conditioned car Luca turned to face Emily, scooted across the seat to take her hands in his. He knew something was wrong, had seen such intense pain in her eyes that his own soul had shrivelled slightly and all he'd wanted was to shield her. 'Would you prefer to go back to the resort?'

Emily shook her head. 'I'm fine.' For a moment he almost believed her. Almost but not quite; her voice was too tight and he knew what he'd seen. 'And I have high hopes of this as a good location.' Her voice held a brightness stark in its falsity and the contrast to the dull shadows, the ache in her brown eyes.

He hesitated, wondered if he should push it, but Emily launched a flow of bright inconsequential chatter as they climbed, interspersed with the constant click of her camera. Not that he could blame her for taking photos; the trek showcased scenery so lushly beautiful it took his breath away.

At one point they made their way through a cardamom plantation. The scent of the spice pervaded the air, supplanted by the waft of tea as they walked through fields of tea. As they got higher a haze of mist added extra atmosphere to the undulating rise and fall of the surrounding hills and valleys.

Once at the peak they sank down, breathless from the walk, and gazed out over the spectacular panoramic view that encompassed so many of Nature's wonders. The flashing blue of a wide river, dense forests that lined the mountain slopes, and the immensity of the sky.

'This is stunning. The sky feels so close that I feel like if I reach up, I can touch it.'

He studied her expression, saw appreciation in her gaze but sadness still shimmered through.

'Emily, tell me what's wrong—I know something has caused you sadness.'

She shook her head. 'It's OK, Luca. I know you don't like to get involved in the emotional side of things. And I *want* to play by your rulebook, want a fun, carefree, magical bubble of time. Turns out it's not that easy to escape reality. What with Ava and now this. But I'll be OK.' She smiled a smile that tore his heartstrings. 'Being up here, the walk, this vista, all seem to bring a tranquillity.'

Luca stilled, listened to her quote his own criteria back at him and castigated himself for being a selfish schmuck. Was that what he wanted from life, to protect himself from another's vulnerability? 'It's not OK,' he said quietly. 'I don't want to play by the rulebook. We have already agreed you are an anomaly. An anomaly in a bubble. So, if you wish to, if I can help, please tell me what has happened.'

There was a silence and as she looked out he knew she was coming to some sort of inner decision.

'Thank you. I would like to tell you; I haven't talked to anyone and up here it feels right to remember what happened.'

Shifting slightly, she leant against him, faced the view, as if she were also sharing her story with the universe. 'I lost my baby,' she said. 'I had a late miscarriage. I was six months pregnant. I thought I was safe, I'd felt him kick, talked to him, played him music. But then I lost him. If I'd gone to term he would have been ten months now, the same age as Amitabh. That's what set me off.'

'I am so sorry.' The words were so inadequate and he pulled her closer, tried to convey his sympathy through the warmth of his body, through closeness. 'I cannot imagine how you must have felt. How you are still feeling.' A year wasn't long enough to get over something like that, if you ever did. 'I am so sorry. For you and for Howard.' The man was a bully, but he didn't deserve to lose a child.

'Howard didn't care—he didn't even want the baby.' Now her face looked pinched, white with remembered strain. 'The baby was an accident but for me he was a happy one. Sure, I had planned to wait a few years, we'd only just got married, but I was still ecstatic. Howard wasn't. He wasn't happy at all. Said it was too early, that a baby would interfere with our happiness. I think he wanted me to consider a termination, but he knew there was no way I would do it. But he resented the baby, hated me being pregnant. The put-downs became more barbed and he kept finding fault with my appearance. Particularly my weight, my skin; the morning sickness disgusted him; he hated that I was tired. He didn't even want anyone to know, said he had an upcoming book release and he didn't want anything to detract from that. So I had to hide the pregnancy.' Now she turned wide eyes onto him. 'And now I keep thinking did I do something wrong? Did I cause the miscarriage by pushing myself when I was tired? By hiding the pregnancy? By dressing wrong— there was a time a few weeks before when I wore high heels. What if that was part of it? If I did something wrong?'

His heart turned in his chest and for a moment anger consumed him, anger at the callous selfishness of her ex-husband. An anger he pushed aside as he heard the torment of guilt in her voice, the fear that it had somehow been her fault.

'Emily, I wasn't there but I know you. You would never put your baby at risk. I bet you did everything right, didn't touch alcohol, ate all the right food, did everything. When my mother was pregnant with Jodi she was exhausted all the time and she pushed and pushed herself.'

'She had to.' Emily's voice was small. 'Maybe I should have stood up to Howard, instead of running around desperately trying to be the perfect wife. I wanted to show him that the baby didn't have to be a bad change in our lives. I thought he loved me.'

Luca pulled her closer to him, could hear the pain and devastation in her voice.

'It turned out he was having an affair. It started whilst I was pregnant—he justified it by saying I had become unattractive, overweight and selfish. I couldn't believe I'd been so stupid. That it had happened to me, that I had believed in him. How could I not have seen the signs? When I watched my mother go through marriage after marriage, I thought I could spot a lie at one hundred paces. But I truly had no idea. How dumb am I?'

'You aren't dumb. Sometimes we believe what we want to believe.'

'Then that makes me a double fool. I grew up watching my mother do that time and again. Believing this man was the one, believing she was loved. And I fell into the same trap. Blown away by the idea that Howard loved the real me. Was interested in me, my photography, my personality—nothing to do with my parents. I thought he loved me for me.'

Luca searched for words of comfort. 'Perhaps he did. My dad loved my mum. Just not enough.'

Emily shook her head. 'Howard didn't love me; I think Howard only loves himself. He wanted the perfect adoring wife. The only reason I believed he loved me was because at least he genuinely didn't care about my parents' fame or fortune. I'd already shown him I was more than ready to adore him, look up to him, listen to him. Then I fell pregnant and he knew he wouldn't be the centre of my world any more. So he cheated on me.'

'Was he sorry?'

'Nope. When I found out I did confront him—he seemed to think his actions were justified as I was no longer attractive. We had a stand-up row. He left and I lost the baby two weeks later.' Now guilt shadowed her eyes again. 'Maybe the row made the difference. I don't know, but I didn't see him again. When I lost the baby it was as if the world collapsed on me. I lost it completely. The past months have been like some sort of nightmare. Howard wanted out, a painless divorce, and I agreed to everything. Then I pretty much went to bed, pulled the duvet over my head and blocked out the world. Turns out you can't do that. Reality creeps in, there are bills to pay and I realised I had to get myself up and going again. The problem is I can't always keep the grief at bay, or the questions. Then I panic. I want to turn the clock back, make different decisions, figure out what I did wrong and fix it.'

'Emily, you did nothing wrong. I know that, I swear it to you. You cannot torture yourself, trying to turn time back, or reliving the past.' He wanted Emily to know he understood. 'When my dad left I spent years trying to figure out why. What I did wrong. All I wanted was a chance to make it right, to turn back time and somehow make him stay. Then I thought if I could figure it out maybe he'd at least visit, call, send a postcard.'

'You did nothing wrong. He did.'

'But it didn't feel like that. Because I know he did love me. I remember the love, sitting on his shoulders, being swung up in the air, bedtime stories, walking along holding his hand. So how could he stop loving me so easily? I must have done something.'

'But you didn't.'

'You didn't do anything wrong either.' Turning away from the view, he focused on her, held her arms gently as she faced him, wanting that connection. 'I know you didn't. You can't second-guess yourself, can't torture yourself with the what-ifs and might-have-beens. Because you can't turn back time, you can't change what happened. But you can remember your baby, honour and cherish his memory. And the joy you felt in him.' Just as perhaps he should cherish his own memories with his dad, the knowledge that for five years he had been loved.

'I did feel joy.' Her eyes were wide now.

'When I knew I was pregnant I felt panic but mostly I felt awe, a deep awe that there was the beginning of a tiny living being growing inside me. I loved tracing his progress, the first small swell of my tummy, the idea that what I ate and drank was helping my baby to develop. Then there was the first time he kicked, the first time I played music to him. I loved him very much. I will always cherish his memory. And however sad I am I need to remember he also gave me joy.' She turned to Luca. 'And I believe your father loved you—you know that, you have all those memories that prove it. You did nothing wrong either, Luca—he did, and I think he regretted it all the days of his life. Yes, he lavished love on Ava, because he didn't want to make the same mistake again. I think he left you and Jodi shares in Dolci in a clumsy way to try to show love and make amends.'

Luca turned and pulled her into a close embrace, touched beyond all reason that in her own pain she could find words to give him comfort. She pulled away gently and said, 'Look.'

He turned his head and watched as the sun started to dip, streaked the sky in a glorious medley of orange and red against the panoramic background of a cloud-streaked sky. The colours seemed to light up the world, dapple and reflect the peaks and valleys, surround them in a magnificent aura of hues and tints.

He moved to pass her the camera but she shook her head. 'I just want to experience this moment. With you.'

So they sat hand in hand and watched the sun set before returning down the slopes, through the plantations and back to the resort and bed, where they held each other in their arms and created a different type of magic.

CHAPTER FOURTEEN

EMILY OPENED HER eyes aware that something wasn't quite right, something was missing. Luca. Groggily she reached out, realised he wasn't there and, after a night spent curled up in his arms or with her head on his chest or spooned up against him with his arm protectively around her, already her body protested at the lack of his skin against hers.

'Hey, sleepyhead.' His deep voice came from the end of the bed and she saw that he was up and dressed in a lightweight suit.

'Good morning.' She stretched. 'It's the meeting with the royal representative,' she remembered.

'That's the one.'

She frowned as she blinked away the last vestiges of sleep. 'You look nervous.' The idea was incongruous—it was hard to imagine nerves daring to impinge anxiety on Luca.

'I've never met a royal rep. But it's not that—

I wanted to make sure you're OK before I leave. Tell you thank you for sharing with me yesterday and I hope you don't regret it.'

Did she? How could she, when he'd shown such understanding, known when to hold her and when to speak, shared his own trauma and loss and feelings with her? Who would have thought it? 'No regrets,' she said. 'So go. You don't want to be late. And good luck—I know this is important to you and I'm sure you'll blow him away.'

Now she'd swear Luca looked…discomfited, uncomfortable, hesitant. Emily propped herself up, her forehead creased in a small frown. 'Is something wrong? You are nervous, aren't you?'

Quickly she swung her legs out of bed, walked towards him, even now revelled in the fact she wore one of his T-shirts, the idea both sexy and intimate. 'Hey. You don't need to worry. I know this endorsement is important to you but I bet you'll nail it.' She reached him and placed her hand on his arm, looked up at him, wanted her words to matter, touched at this unexpected vulnerability. 'Truly. Your chocolate is fabulous and endorsing it will give the royal family and Jaipura some great publicity. All you need to do is tell the truth.'

She'd swear he flinched, the idea confirmed

as he took a step back, away from her touch, and a sudden hurt mingled with foreboding.

'Luca? Did I say something wrong?'

A succinct curse dropped from his lips. 'No. You said nothing wrong at all. You're right,' he said. 'I do need to tell the truth. To you.'

'What do you mean?'

He gestured to the table by the window. 'Why don't we sit?'

Emily frowned and the temptation to refuse, to simply cover her ears and go *la-la-la*, nigh on overwhelmed her. But instead she leant down, scooped up the trousers she'd discarded the night before and pulled them on, suddenly feeling at a disadvantage in the T-shirt.

She followed him to the table and sat in the wicker chair opposite him.

'I don't understand. What truth?'

'My meeting with the royal representative. I didn't make it to get an endorsement for my chocolate.' His voice was even, matter of fact, as if now he had decided to tell the truth, whatever that meant, he would do so calmly. The only tell was the clench of his jaw, and the hand through his hair. 'Or rather that isn't my prime objective.'

'Then what is?' Emily closed her eyes for a second, tried to figure out what the hell was going on. A sense of foreboding rippled in her gut, one she tried to calm. There would be an explanation for this, a good one, one that would assuage the sense of doom.

'I want to find out some information about Jodi.'

'Your sister Jodi? I'm still not with you.' What did Jodi have to do with anything?

'Jodi was badly impacted by our father's death. She decided to take some time out and go travelling and to begin with she loved it. She kept in touch, sent photos, we called regularly. Then she came to Jalpura, visited the cocoa farm, and got involved in organising the film festival. Then everything changed, her messages became less frequent and she sounded different. I can't explain it, but I knew something was wrong even if she wouldn't admit it. Then she left Jalpura and pretty much went incommunicado. She said she needed some space and I shouldn't worry or pull any big-brother shit.'

Now concern for Jodi outweighed her own confusion. 'So have you found out anything about Jodi? When did you last hear from her?'

'All I found out was that whilst she was working on the film festival she made friends with royalty. A princess.'

Emily raised her eyebrows. 'So either Princess Alisha or Princess Riya. I did some research partly to help you with the endorsement, but also as part of my plan to bring a flavour of royalty into the campaign.'

'Yes, that's what I figure. So I was hoping Pradesh Patankar could shed some light, maybe give me an idea of what happened to Jodi.'

The idea that he was willing to do all this for his sister touched her, more so because she knew no one in her family would ever do that for her. 'So you came to Jalpura to find out what happened.' Her voice was small, because, however much she lauded his concern for his sister, Luca had lied to her by omission. Worse. 'The advertising campaign was a cover.'

'No. The campaign is real.'

'But you only did it now because it gave you a reason to come to Jalpura.'

He hesitated, rocked back on his feet as he looked away from her and then back. 'Yes.'

'Why didn't you tell me?'

'Because I couldn't betray Jodi's trust; she would hate for me to discuss her private stuff with anyone, let alone...'

'Ava's best friend,' Emily completed. And in a way she could see that, understood that he couldn't possibly have told her about this when he first met her. But it still didn't make sense. 'In which case, why me? Why did you bring me here? Why would *you* employ Ava's best friend? Then bring me here.'

She stared at him, saw the discomfort in his stance, in his expression, and once again he looked away.

'Luca?'

Now cold hard premonition froze inside her and she wrapped her arms around herself, knew that, bad as this already was, it was about to become worse.

'I thought your name would help.'

'My name?' The penny dropped with a resounding leaden clang as everything fell into place. It all made sense now. Why Luca was neither bothered about seeing her portfolio nor cared about her lack of experience. 'You hired me for my name.' She started to pace, needed to move, to stoke the anger that she knew preceded the burn of utter, complete humiliation. 'It wouldn't have mattered how useless a photographer I was, you needed me here, on Jalpura, because of my name. You thought it would open doors for you.' Hurt began to cascade through her along with mortification. Luca hadn't believed in her talent, hadn't hired her because of her photography skills. He'd hired her because her name might have helped in his quest for Jodi.

Her brain clouded, fogged with hurt, and she tried to cleave through. Luca had decided to come to Jalpura to look for his sister, had decided to come here under cover of a photo shoot and bring Emily Khatri with him. In case she could be of use. Correction. In case her name could be of use. However, he'd failed to apprise her of the fact and she hadn't realised that was part of the deal.

What a fool she was, to have believed the whole spiel. Had she really believed that Luca's judgement was correct, could miraculously negate Howard's? Howard had been a cheat and a liar, turned out so was Luca.

'Why?' she asked quietly now. 'Why did you sleep with me, Luca? What was that? Some sort of bonus, a way of passing time in between your investigations? A way of distracting me in case I figured something out?' Because with hindsight she could see that he hadn't ever really engaged with the campaign. They'd visited locations but they'd never sat down and discussed ideas or brainstormed. Instead they'd spent their time talking, getting up close and personal.

'No. This. Us. It's real.' He gestured between them, his voice taut.

She shook her head, as a memory engulfed her of Howard being confronted with his infidelity and the way he had dismissed it. *'Lucille was an interim woman. Whilst you're pregnant. She doesn't mean anything. You. Me. We're real.'*

Disbelief at her own stupidity churned her

tummy. Again—she'd done it again. Been taken in by an illusion. With Howard she'd believed he loved her for herself. With Luca she'd believed he'd employed her because he had faith in her talent, in her photographic skills. Had also believed he cared, that these days were magical. In reality they had been just another arrangement.

With Howard she'd believed in their marriage, been worried about how he was adjusting to fatherhood, run around trying to make things right. Whilst all the time he'd been sleeping with someone else. With Luca she'd believed in his ad campaign, was convinced he'd believed in her. Humiliation, mortification at her own stupidity, roiled over her skin, tinged and patched it with cold, and she rubbed her hands up and down her arms. Oh, God, she'd confided in him, slept with him…trusted him with her deepest emotions. Told him about her baby. She came to a halt in front of where he stood.

'No, it's not real, Luca.' Any more than her marriage had been. 'Everything, all of this, what happened between us, is fake. Founded on a lie.' She shook her head. 'I need to go.' She'd reached the door when she heard his voice.

'Emily. No. Wait. Please.'

From somewhere Luca found his voice. For the past minutes he'd been rooted to the spot, frozen as her words punched into him, each one a sucker punch to his ribs, his chest, his heart. Regret, panic and a fear he couldn't understand all churned inside him as the impact of his actions washed over him in a cold wave.

Slowly she turned and he took a step towards her, stopped at her instinctive recoil. How could he blame her? He'd messed up big time and he had no idea how to put it right.

'I am sorry. So sorry. But when I met you and you came up with the idea for the ad to be shot on Jalpura it seemed like a brilliant idea. A win-win situation. A way to help Jodi and achieve an amazing ad campaign. That was always real, and I did believe you were the perfect person for the job.'

'Because of my name.' The bitterness in her voice was justified. And unanswerable and that knowledge unleashed a sense of panic inside him, a realisation that this was sliding out of his control. Had it been just hours ago that they had been lying entwined, she with her head on his chest, cocooned in his arms? Enough. Somehow he had to explain his actions, convince Emily what they had was real, that the bubble was intact.

'Yes, your name mattered, but the ad campaign is real—your talent is real.'

'But you wouldn't have hired me if it wasn't for my name.'

He could see the dullness in her eyes and he wished, how he wished, he could turn the clock back and make this right.

He exhaled, knew he owed her that truth. 'I don't know the answer to that. But if I hadn't it would have been because you are Ava's friend—not because I didn't believe you could do the job.'

'That makes it worse, Luca. All my life I've been someone's something. My parents' daughter, Howard's wife. Ava's friend. I thought—' She broke off and lifted her hands to her cheeks.

He knew what she'd thought. 'You thought that with me you were yourself.'

'Yes, and now I know I wasn't.'

'But you were. The past few days—they have been magical. What happened between us is nothing to do with your name. Every word I said about your talent is the God's honest truth.'

'I want to believe you, but I don't. Not when the whole trip here was based on a lie.' She shook her head. 'I can just about understand why you did what you did at the start. I understand you love your sister and you put her first.' The words a stark reminder to him that no one ever put her first. Not her mother, or her father. Certainly not Howard. Had she believed Luca would? 'If you were going to keep that from me, then you shouldn't have got involved with me, shouldn't have let me think this was something it never was. I bared my soul to you—and the whole time you were lying to me.'

'I told you things I have never shared with anyone. The only thing I did not tell you about was Jodi.'

'But that omission made all the difference.'

She was right and the knowledge that he'd hurt a woman who was already hurting so much, added to the burden she already carried, twisted inside him. The realization he'd done it again— once again he'd pushed away a person he loved through his own misguided actions. Only this time he knew exactly what he'd done wrong and no amount of wishing could undo that.

Whoa. Love? The realisation caused him to let out a small sigh of disbelief even as he knew it to be true. He loved Emily and he'd screwed it up. Of course, he had. Cold, clammy awareness roiled. This was exactly why he'd made rules and regulations, had only committed to those immutable long-term arrangements. Where he couldn't hurt anyone or get hurt himself. Because he'd known all along that he could not manage love, had no idea how to keep it, navigate it.

He'd already hurt Emily, in a few 'magical

days'. Because now the magic had turned dark and God only knew what harm and pain he'd manage to inflict over time. This had to end, and end now.

'You're right. I messed up and I'm sorry. Sorry I hurt you and sorry I failed you. I know there is no need for you to believe this, but I do believe in your talent. I believe in you. Please don't let my stupidity hurt you and please take care of yourself.'

She nodded, ran her hands up and down her arms and he had to fight not to step forward and pull her into his arms.

'I hope you find Jodi and that she is OK.' She took a deep breath. 'If you need to use my name, use it. If you need me to do something to help you gain access to the royal family, then please let me know.' The idea that she would make this offer flayed him and he knew that not even for Jodi would he ask Emily to do that. The knowledge was both ironic and surprising. 'I will write up my ideas and a report for your marketing department to file away, should you ever decide to go ahead with the campaign.' Her words were as jerky and stilted as his had been and he clenched his hands into fists. 'There are plenty of photographers who will jump at the chance.'

He stood frozen to the spot as the door clicked

shut and his heart cracked. Part of him wanted to run after her, to beg forgiveness, declare his love, but he knew there was no point. That way could only end in more hurt to Emily. And he'd hurt her enough. With his inadequacy, his sheer selfishness,. There was no defence for what he'd done. Yes, he had prioritised Jodi, because he had vowed he would never let his sister down as his father had done. But in so doing he had let Emily down instead—a knowledge that seared him even as his whole being yearned for her. But there was no point. People he loved left him. End of.

He didn't know how long he remained there still and silent inhaling her elusive scent, the evocative floral tang that lingered in the air and filled him with an ache of regret and guilt. *Fool.* At some point he turned his head, caught a glimpse of her hairbrush on the bedside table and an image of her pulling it through the sheer satin of her hair caught his breath in bereft that he'd never see that again.

CHAPTER FIFTEEN

Five days later, Turin

LUCA SAT BEHIND his office desk and looked at the email, read it again.

Dear Luca

I wanted to let you know that I have found out some information about Jodi. After our conversation I contacted the royal representative and used my name to gain access to the Queen, who is a huge fan of my father. Whilst I was there I also met with the younger members of the family. I asked about Jodi but they all claimed not to have met her.

However, the following day Princess Alisha contacted me to tell me that in fact she does know Jodi. She was going under a different name of Gemma Lewes. The Princess only knows her real name because she sneaked a look at her passport. She says she and Jodi became good friends, but she left Jalpura very abruptly and has only responded to messages to thank Alisha for her friendship, apologise for leaving without saying goodbye and to say she will be in touch.

I hope Jodi is OK. I have posted you a report outlining my ideas for the ad campaign, a storyboard and a selection of photographs.

Emily

As he gazed down at the screen instead of the text he could see Emily's face, could picture her expression as she typed, the fierce stare as she weighed each word, the way she'd tuck her hair behind her ear. And now memories streamed: the sweetness of her smile, the way her eyes lit up with laughter, sparked with anger or desire. The way she crinkled her nose in question or doubt. And then the memory of her face on that final morning zinged into his mind, the hurt, the way she had wrapped her arms around herself for protection. From the hurt he'd caused.

Come on, Luca. Focus.

He forced his mind to Jodi, to his sister. To *his* meeting with the royal representative. Pradesh Patankar had said he'd never heard of Jodi Petrovelli. That would be explained by the alias that Jodi had for some reason assumed. But whatever his sister was doing it was clear she wanted to be left alone by friends and family alike. Exactly as she had said all along. Because Jodi knew she could count on him, on their mother. If she needed them, they would be there.

Emily didn't have that. Her parents were useless, prioritised others over her. She had Ava but she couldn't turn to her because she'd promised not to tell Ava about them and instinctively Luca knew she would keep that promise.

Rising, he picked up his jacket and headed for the door, phone in hand as he called an airline to book a flight to London. A few hours later he approached Dolci headquarters, entered and was shown up to Ava's office.

'Luca?' Ava rose from behind her desk and walked round, a smile on her face, but worry in her eyes. 'Is everything OK? You said it was urgent.'

'It is to me. Thank you for seeing me at such short notice.'

'It's not a problem. You're family. Why don't you sit down? I'll grab us a coffee and you can tell me what is going on.'

Luca sat, knew that his own pride was a small price to pay. Ava was Emily's best friend and Emily deserved to have support from her. 'I messed up,' he told his sister. 'And I want to put it right. But now please go to Emily. I think she needs a friend.'

* * *

Emily sat at her desk in her London apartment and looked down at the photos spread out in front of her. The photos she'd taken in Jalpura. Taken *after* the last time with Luca, when she'd moved into a hostel for a few days, met with the royal representative, before she'd returned to London. In that time she'd taken refuge in photography, had taken photos to try and distract herself from the pain. To try to make her stop missing Luca.

Memories caused tears to sting her eyes and she tried for at least the millionth time to banish Luca from her mind. Didn't understand how Luca seemed to have distilled into her whole being. Why images of him continued to pervade her mind, waking and sleeping, memories to cascade through her. Of his smile, his touch, the spikiness of his hair, the feel of him… *Enough.* No more thoughts of Luca. He was not for her; he had lied to her.

For his sister.

Jeez, Emily. Stop thinking about the man. She didn't even understand why her deluded mind was making excuses for him.

Emily picked up her cup of tea and forced her attention to the photos. She focused on the simple picture of a Jalpuran woman teaching her child how to cook, and she felt a small curl of pride. The photograph conveyed so much—the love between mother and child, the simplicity of the earthenware pot, the youth of the child, the bright colour of the lentils being measured into the pan, the light and heat reflected off the stainless-steel plates.

A photo she would never have had the courage to take if it weren't for Luca.

Her eyes scanned the remaining photos and her gut told her she'd done something good, captured an essence of Jalpura and the richness of its life, culture and people. But then doubt surfaced—how could she trust her gut when she'd been so wrong about Luca? His voice rang in her head. 'Believe in yourself.' Wasn't that what they had both told each other?

The ring of her doorbell interrupted her thoughts. Who could that be? Stupid hope touched her that it would be Luca. *Ridiculous.* Luca would be on Jalpura now, talking to the Princess, tracking Jodi down.

Rising, she went to the door and pulled it open. 'Ava?'

'Hello, lovely. Are you OK? I came as soon as Luca told me.'

Emily froze. 'Luca told you what?' she said cautiously.

'He turned up at my office, said he'd messed

up, he thought you may need a friend. That he needed to make it right. Then he left.'

'Left?'

'Yes.' Ava entered and enveloped her friend in a hug. 'Tell me what happened.'

Emily tried to think, hugged her friend back and then stepped back. What was going on? Why had Luca gone to Ava?

Ava studied her best friend's expression. 'OMG. Have you fallen for Luca? And vice versa?'

'No. Of course not.'

Had she? No, she'd fallen for an illusion, a fake. A man who'd only employed her for her name, had conned her. A man who had listened to her, encouraged her, held her whilst she cried and made love to her. Love…that was what it had felt like; their time together had felt full of love and caring and light and laughter. She loved him; it was so obvious, so clear…so disastrous. What was she going to do? Could something that had felt so real really have been nothing more than a con?

Ava stepped forward. 'Hey, it's going to be all right.'

Was it? And what had Luca meant about putting things right?

Luca rang the bell of the enormous whitewashed house, congratulated himself that he had managed to gain entry to the house of Rajiv Khatri. It had taken a certain level of determination to get through to the man himself but eventually he had succeeded, and once Rajiv believed he genuinely wanted to talk about Emily he had agreed to a meeting.

The door swung open to reveal a stately butler who studied Luca's credentials and then led the way through a spacious hallway to an enormous lounge, filled with sofas and family paraphernalia. The room was a mix of style and comfort.

Minutes later a tall slender Indian man walked in, dressed in jeans and a T-shirt, with a cautious smile on his face. 'Good morning.'

'Good morning.'

'Would you like refreshments? Tea? Coffee.'

Luca declined and the Bollywood actor gestured for him to be seated and followed suit. 'So you wish to speak with me about Emily?'

'Yes.' Somewhat belatedly Luca realised he should maybe have prepared better for this, had been so focused on getting in front of Rajiv he hadn't planned what to say. 'When is the last time you saw her?'

The actor frowned. 'I am afraid I don't see what business it is of yours.'

Luca forced his body to relax; he was here to act as an intermediary, not an accuser. Part of him knew that he was maybe overstepping, but he knew Emily would never take either parent to task and someone had to.

'You're right and I apologise.' Luca inhaled deeply. 'I am here because recently I…got to know your daughter and I know it saddens her that…you aren't close. That because you have a second family who you live with, you never needed to get close to her.'

'That isn't tr—'

'Yes, it is.' A quiet voice intervened and, turning, Luca saw that a petite Indian woman had entered the room, dressed in a light blue patterned salwar kameez. 'Hello, Mr Petrovelli. I am Neela Khatri, mother to the second family.'

Rajiv rose when he saw his wife, but his expression was still one of anger. 'I have always treated Emily like family. She was only a baby when her mother and I split but I made sure I had proper visitation rights and when I moved back here… I…'

'Stop, Rajiv.' Neela spoke quietly as she moved over to her husband and took his hand in hers. 'Let us listen to what he has to say.' She gestured to Luca, who tried to gather his words together, as sudden panic assailed him. Perhaps he was making this worse, and Rajiv Khatri would withdraw all support.

'Please do not be angry with Emily. She has

no idea I am here, so if I am speaking out of turn please blame me. Emily has not uttered a word of anger or blame. She is just sad. Sad that she can't be part of your extended family, doesn't have a close bond with any of you.'

Rajiv's expression changed, the frown indicative of a man who was listening, but it was Neela who spoke.

'I am sorry,' she said simply. 'Some of the blame is mine. To begin with I saw Emily as a threat, a reminder of Marigold, and I believed that you still loved her, had married me on the rebound.'

Now Rajiv took his wife's other hand in his and they exchanged a smile. 'And now?' he asked.

'Now I know you love me.' The look the couple exchanged was so full of love and understanding that Luca blinked, wondered if Emily's belief that this marriage was based on affection alone could be wrong. Neela smiled at her husband. 'But the pattern had been set and we were so caught up in our family that Emily must have felt excluded.'

Neela turned back to Luca. 'Please continue.'

'I think Emily would like to feel she is important to you, that she comes first, that she isn't on the sidelines of your lives. She has had a hard time lately and she could do with some support.'

Rajiv nodded his head. 'Thank you for this intervention. I will speak with Emily.' He shook his head. 'No, I will do better than that. I will go and see my daughter and try to make things right.'

Luca smiled, tried to imagine Emily's face when she saw her father, hoped with all his heart that they would work out a way to forge a new relationship. Hoped that when he met with Marigold, Emily's mother would react positively as well.

'Thank you,' he said.

Neela shook her head. 'It is we who thank you. For doing this for Emily.'

A week later

Emily tried to salvage as much of her courage as she could, even as nerves coiled inside her like a mass of writhing snakes. As her high heels clicked across the London street her heart pounded her ribs so hard she feared it would burst through.

Her mind still spun over the events of the past days. A few days after Ava's visit her doorbell had rung again and this time as she'd opened the door she'd nearly fainted. Had found it difficult to believe the evidence of her eyes, as she took in the identity of her visitors. Her parents, both of them *together* on the doorstep. The next hours had been both emotional and rewarding and had left her filled with hope that perhaps she and her parents could forge new bonds.

When they had left Emily had emailed Luca to thank him and he'd replied. The words were embossed on her mind.

Dear Emily,

I am glad that it worked out. I was wondering if you would be able to meet with me, though I will fully understand if that is not something you want to do. I would like to talk.

If you feel you can do this perhaps we could meet for a cocktail in London at your convenience?

Best wishes,

Luca

So here she was.

She slowed down as she reached her destination, knew that she would regret it to her dying day if she turned tail and ran now. A deep breath, and she pushed the door open, blinked as she entered the dimly lit interior and realised the place was empty.

No, not empty. As she approached the bar she saw Luca and her head whirled. She halted in her tracks, soaked in his sheer masculine beauty, every familiar angle and plane, the dark hair a little overlong now, his stance alert and almost primal as his eyes scanned the door.

'Luca.'

'Emily.'

Unbidden happiness fizzed inside her and she wanted to hurl herself into his arms, wanted to hold and be held, inhale his scent... Instead she stepped forward, approached the bar, half relieved, half disappointed at the barrier between them.

'I wasn't sure if you'd come.' His voice was low, deep and so wonderfully familiar.

'Neither was I. But...' she looked round '... where is everyone?'

Now he smiled and she was transported back to Jalpura, to Turin, to all the times his face had lit up her world. 'I've bought the bar.'

'You've bought it?'

'Yup. I am going to open a cocktail bar in London. Palazzo di Cioccolato is branching out. I listened to what you said, and I've done some serious thinking. I do want to launch in London and I will, but not yet. Perhaps when it is possible to come to a decision about Dolci, perhaps then. But in the meantime I realised I was so focused on rivalling Dolci that maybe I missed out on doing the other things I wanted to do. I like mixing cocktails, I enjoyed working at Silvio's. So here we are. Welcome to Teepee.'

Emily thought and smiled as she got it. 'Teepee—or TP as in Therese Petrovelli.'

'Yup. My mum loves the idea.'

'So do I.' Happiness for him swept through her, that he'd started to move on from revenge, from the emotional turmoil caused by James's actions in life and death. Yet the happiness was tinged with sadness, because she'd hoped Luca had wanted to see her for something different.

He cleared his throat. 'I hoped you would stay and have the very first cocktail served here.'

'I'd like that. I wanted to talk to you as well.' She sat down at the bar. 'I want to thank you. For going to my parents. I'm not sure exactly what you said but it's made a world of difference; opened up a whole new facet to my relationship with both of them.'

'I'm glad. Truly glad.'

'I think things will be different from now on. They actually turned up together, said it was their way of showing me that they truly wanted to try and change things up. I'm going to spend some time in Mumbai with my dad on our own and then stay with the family. My mum said she knows she can't change the past but she hopes she and I can spend a lot of time together and she offered to not go to Derek's—her current husband's—film premiere so she could be with me instead. I told her there was no need, but I appreciated the offer. Anyway, she took me on a girls' day out—hence the new look.' She glanced down at her outfit, aware she was talking too much but she couldn't stop. 'We had a lot of fun...massages, spa, shopping and lunch. So it's a start. Thank you.'

Because right now, whatever happened with her parents, she knew that Luca had gone the extra mile to do something for her. And that sent an appreciative glow through her veins.

'There is no need to thank me. I wanted to do that. For you.'

The expression on his face was so genuine, so warm, that something melted inside her, urged her to throw caution to the wind and vault over the bar into his arms. No way. That would embarrass them both and there had been enough mortification to last her a lifetime. She tucked a strand of hair behind her ear. 'I was wondering—have you managed to track Jodi down? Did you meet with the Princess?'

'No on both counts.'

Surprise widened her eyes. 'Oh... I assumed...'

'Once I got your email I realised exactly what I needed to do and I did it. I went to see Ava and then I flew to Mumbai to talk to your father, then I went to see your mother and here we are.'

'But…'

Luca shook his head. 'I will, of course, try to speak with the Princess and continue my search for Jodi. But in the end Jodi is an adult and she knows she can turn to me or our mum any time she needs to. I knew you were hurting and I wanted to—'

'Put me first.' The realisation cascaded over her skin and her heart sang.

'Yes. Because that's what you deserve, Emily. To be put first. And you didn't deserve what I did. I should have been upfront.'

Now she reached out, a small tentative touch of his arm, revelled in the familiar hardness of muscle under her fingers. 'It's OK. I understand why you did it. You love your sister and you couldn't take the risk that I wouldn't help.'

'That is the reason but that doesn't make it right. Not when it hurt you, not when it made you doubt that everything else between us was real. Because it was real, Emily. All of it. I meant every word. I believe in your talent, I believe in you. I hold your grief about your baby in my own heart. Because I love you.'

There was a silence and her heart fluttered in her chest. 'You love me?' The words seemed impossible, words she knew he'd vowed to never say again. Yet she knew them to be true, knew this man would never say those words unless he meant them with all his heart. Because he knew the power of love, the immensity of the gift and the responsibility that went with it. For Luca love meant a promise to never leave, never abandon the other.

'Yes, I do. I love you, with all my heart and soul. I know you may not love me back, but I want you to know how I feel. I love you. I love your courage and your strength in the face of the grief and pain you have faced. I love your sense of humour, your grace, the way you smile. I love how you feel in my arms when I wake up. I love how caring you are and how you see the world. Whether it is from behind a lens or not. I love you.'

Words welled up inside her, but she knew the most important ones. 'I love you too, Luca. With all my heart.'

She watched as he absorbed the words and then *he* vaulted across the bar and pulled her close, twirled her round and then gently placed her down, still safely encircled in his arms. 'Are you sure? After what I did?'

'I understand what you did. Yes, it was wrong, but you also did so much that was right—you started my healing process, you made me believe in myself, listened to me, held me and you made me happy.'

His silver-grey eyes lit up. 'I appreciate that—

that you have found it in you to absolve me. Because I know what I did was indefensible; I regret it with all my heart. The idea that I hurt you, hurt the woman I love. It will not happen again. I promise you I will never lie to you again, not by omission or fact. If there is something difficult to face up to…'

'Then we will do it together.'

'Yes.'

'I did not know it was possible to be this happy.' He tipped her chin up with his finger. 'To know I will see your face every day when I wake up and last thing before I go to sleep.'

She looked up at him, gave a small mischievous smile. 'But surely you would prefer a different arrangement? One where we only see each other every blue moon.'

'No. I would emphatically not prefer that.' He tugged her closer. 'The idea makes my blood run cold.' Now his face became serious. 'You changed me, Emily. When my father died I felt such an influx of emotions, and I didn't know what to do with them. I wanted to bury them; you helped me to face them. I felt as though I had failed because I hadn't got my revenge. You showed me it was OK to feel and how to channel that emotion, to genuinely believe it wasn't my fault he left. You showed me that talking about how you feel is a good thing. That feeling is a good thing. You taught me that spending time with someone, getting closer, is a risk worth taking, is fun and rewarding. Today you have shown me it is possible for me to make a mistake, do wrong and still be loved. My actions did not drive you away for ever.'

'No. Because you also did so many caring things: you helped me grieve my baby, you convinced me that Howard was wrong about my talent, you showed me how to stand up to his voice in my head, you helped me move forward when I never thought I could. When we left London for Turin I panicked because I thought I couldn't leave my home, my grief—it felt like a betrayal of my baby. With you I learnt to laugh again, to dance, to work. To grow. You made me believe in myself, made me want to pursue my own dreams.'

His arms tightened around her. 'I want to have children with you, when you're ready. I know it will take time. And we will never forget your first baby. I will cherish his memory with you. As I will always cherish you.'

Her heart seemed to wrench with happiness. 'And our children will be the luckiest in the world to have a dad like you. I know you will always be there for them, for every milestone.'

'We will be there for them and I think we

will be the happiest family in the world. I love you, Emily.'

'I love you too, Luca.' She knew she would never get tired of saying the words of love.

'I think now is the perfect moment for that cocktail I promised you.' Taking her hand, he pulled her round to the opposite side of the bar. 'These are the ingredients. Tequila for strength, pineapple juice for sweetness, rum to add a little spice, and chilli for a bit of heat and some shavings of chocolate for extra sweetness.'

She watched as he expertly set to work, absorbed every deft movement as he mixed and shook the ingredients, allowed her gaze to linger on every inch of his glorious body, full of joy that this beautiful, generous, caring man was hers for life.

Now he smiled at her, the smile so full of love that she could feel it envelop her as he handed her the glass, expertly garnished and complete with an umbrella.

'Hold on. I need to get the *aperitivo*.' He returned a few minutes later. 'I thought we could have dessert first.'

His voice had a small catch in it and Emily glanced across at him, saw a sparkle in his eye, but also a hint of nerves as he placed down a plate with a variety of truffles, in individual paper cases, beautifully arranged in a pyramid.

He picked up his cocktail and they clinked glasses. 'To us,' he said.

'To us.' She looked at the drink. 'It's beautiful.'

'Yes. As is the woman who inspired it. Would you like to know what it is called?' His voice had dipped to a husky rumble that slid over her skin, made her giddy as it seemed so full of promise.

'What is it called?'

'Emily's proposal,' he said, and her heart beat a little faster as he nodded to the plate. 'Take the top chocolate.'

She did so, felt the weight of it and now her pulse rate notched up as she picked up the chocolate and gasped. Nestled in the paper case was a ring.

Luca reached out and took it, went down on one knee.

'Emily Khatri, I love you with all my heart. I swear to cherish and look after you, stand by your side through thick and thin, for the rest of my life. Will you marry me?'

Tears of happiness prickled her eyelids as she nodded. 'I will marry you, Luca. And I vow to always be there for you. For ever.'

He slipped the ring onto her finger and she gazed down at it. 'It's beautiful.' The glitter of white diamonds alternated with some brown gemstones she didn't recognise.

His grin widened. 'They are called chocolate diamonds,' he explained, and she gave a small gurgle of laughter.

'Of course, they are—and they are perfect.' Just as she knew their life together would be.

* * * * *

If you missed the previous story in the The Casseveti Inheritance trilogy, then check out

Italian Escape with the CEO

And if you enjoyed this story, check out these other great reads from Nina Milne

Baby on the Tycoon's Doorstep
Their Christmas Royal Wedding
Whisked Away by Her Millionaire Boss

All available now!